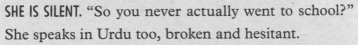

SHE IS SILENT. "So you never actually went to school?" She speaks in Urdu too, broken and hesitant.

I take a deep breath. There's no use getting angry. It's a reality I can't escape. "Poor people have to work. We don't have the luxury of school."

"I . . . I . . ." She switches to English. "I'm so sorry."

I blink away the fierceness from my eyes. This is good, I remind myself. She's feeling sorry for me, which means she may help me. "I'll be okay now you are here," I tell her firmly. "You can teach me English."

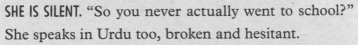

a Thousand Questions

Saadia Faruqi

Quill Tree Books
An Imprint of HarperCollins Publishers

Quill Tree Books is an imprint of HarperCollins Publishers

Library of Congress Cataloging-in-Publication Data

Names: Faruqi, Saadia, author.
Title: A thousand questions / Saadia Faruqi.
Description: First edition. | New York, NY : HarperCollins Children's
    Books, [2020] | Audience: Ages 8–12. | Audience: Grades 4–6. |
    Summary: Told in two voices, eleven-year-olds Mimi, who is visiting her
    wealthy grandparents in Karachi, Pakistan, for the first time and Sakina,
    daughter of the grandparents' cook, form an unexpected friendship.
Identifiers: LCCN 2020000866 | ISBN 978-0-06-294321-7 (paperback)
Subjects: CYAC: Friendship—Fiction. | Americans—Pakistan—Fiction.
    | Household employees—Fiction. | Grandparents—Fiction. | Single-
    parent families—Fiction. | Family life—Pakistan—Fiction. | Karachi
    (Pakistan)—Fiction. | Pakistan—Fiction.
Classification: LCC PZ7.1.F373 Tho 2020 | DDC [Fic]—dc23
LC record available at https://lccn.loc.gov/2020000866

Typography by David Curtis
22 23 24 25 26   PC/BRR   10 9 8 7 6 5 4 3 2 1
❖
First trade paperback edition, 2022

For all the girls of Pakistan,
who live with courage,
conviction, and passion.
I see you.

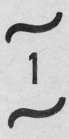

MIMI
SUMMER VACATION IS OVERRATED

Imagine an oven, like 400 degrees. Then imagine crawling inside and closing the door behind you. That's what Pakistan feels like in the summer. Who'd be dumb enough to crawl inside a superhot oven, you ask?

Good question. Nobody with brains, that's who.

We're standing outside the Jinnah Airport in Karachi, trying to get a taxi from a small kiosk with dirty windows. There are a million people around me, all talking faster than I can understand, and anyway they're talking in Urdu so I have only a vague idea of what they're saying. Mom fans herself with a *Parents* magazine, the blonde model on the cover all creased as she tries to keep her mom-cool. I try fanning too, but my copy of the new Dork Diaries is too thick and short to give me any air. "Ugh!" I grunt, and Mom turns to frown at me.

"No complaining, Mimi," she reminds me, patting my nose with her finger. That's been our rule since I was a little girl. No complaining, no matter how hard things get. Not when Dad left us when I was five. Not when I crashed my bike in the street outside our Houston apartment at age seven and broke my leg in three places. Not when Mom lost her teaching job at the Houston Art Institute last year and went on a million interviews, always returning with a smile on her tired face, saying, "It's fine. Something will turn up soon."

But this forced vacation in Pakistan, the land of my ancestors . . . This is not the something I'd been expecting to turn up.

I swat angrily at a big fly that's been trying to land on my face for the last ten minutes. "Not easy," I hiss at Mom. The fly glares at me with its hundred eyes, daring me to catch it.

Mom turns back and offers an apologetic smile to the man in the window. "So how much?" she asks in Urdu. I can't speak it too well, but I've heard it enough to know what she's saying. How much to go to Grandma and Grandpa's house?

That's another thing. I've never even met these Pakistani grandparents of mine. Mom's parents. They call us on Skype once in a while, but mostly in the middle of the night, when I'm already asleep, because of the time difference. I have to stay up late on my birthday to talk to them, but it's always an awkward moment when they stare at me through cyberspace. A stern woman with glasses and arched eyebrows. A man with a shock of white hair and twinkling eyes.

Mom is still haggling with the man in the kiosk. He says something, and she shakes her head. "Too much, that's insane!" she says, firm and clear.

"It's nothing in dollars, ma'am," he tells her firmly, almost mocking. I gasp. How does he know we're American? Is it my Old Navy backpack, or my colorful Skechers sneakers? Is it Mom's dangly earrings or her white embroidered tunic worn over jeans? I'm pretty sure it's the clothes. I survey the women milling around us. Almost everyone is dressed in shalwar kameez of a dizzying variety of colors. Blues and greens like the ocean. Reds and yellows like the leaves in fall.

I do have the traditional Pakistani dress, a black linen kameez with silver embroidery on the sleeves and a plain white cotton shalwar that's too short for my legs now. I wore it twice last year for the two Eid celebrations, and then stuffed it in the back of my closet. I prefer jeans and T-shirts with funny messages. Right now, for instance, I'm wearing a white T-shirt with a purple poop emoji. It's holding its nose and asking *WHAT STINKS?*

I can smell so many things at the moment, none of them good. Garbage spoiling in the early sun. Sweat. Muddy shoes. My T-shirt suddenly doesn't seem that funny. I take my blue cardigan from around my waist and put it on over the poop emoji. "What do you think the temperature is, Mom?" I ask. "Probably a hundred degrees. Or do they use Celsius here?"

Mom shushes me with a finger. She and the man in the kiosk have decided on a price. I never knew one could haggle over taxi fares. Another man walks out, picks up our luggage, and takes it to a white sedan with a broken bumper, covered in dust, and we climb in. "Thank you," I say in English, and he stares at me.

"Is it okay to say thank you?" I whisper to Mom as we settle in and the driver starts the taxi slowly, honking the horn every few seconds to alert people on the road. Wait, is this a road or the sidewalk? It's hard to tell because there are people everywhere.

Mom gives me the side-eye. "Please, can we take a break from your thousands of questions, just this once?"

"Mo-om!"

She leans her head back and closes her eyes. "Yes, Mimi, you can say thank you. Or shukriya."

"Really? I feel like that guy didn't understand me

when I said thank you to him. Or maybe he's just not used to getting thanked. What do you think?"

She doesn't reply. "Mom?" I say, louder, then feel the driver's eyes on me in the rearview mirror.

"Just look out the window, sweetie," Mom murmurs. "You don't want to miss any details for your travel journal, do you?"

I grimace, thinking of the journal Mom gave me a few weeks before we left Houston. I'm secretly planning to write to Dad about my trip, even though I haven't heard from him in years, but she doesn't need to know that. Somehow I doubt she'll be thrilled. She always mutters about him and says "good riddance to bad rubbish" or something like that if anyone asks. But maybe if I write to him, he'll start writing back.

I turn toward the window, shutting my mouth firmly. At least the car isn't too hot. The crowds outside have disappeared, and we're cruising down a big road with neat little trees on each side. The traffic is heavy, though. There are small cars, motorcycles with loads of passengers, and big buses with men sitting on the tops and hanging from the sides. Billboards line the sides of the roads, advertising everything from the latest fashions to cell phone service. A few signs in English proclaim *DON'T FORGET TO VOTE ON AUGUST 1*, with dozens of Pakistani flags surrounding the words.

My eyes are literally popping out of my head; I can feel them. It's all so strange, but also cool and bright, an explosion of color so sharp it reaches inside me and draws out a little sigh.

I realize I'm pressing my face against the window and force myself to sit back and relax. This is Karachi, the largest city in Pakistan, the birthplace of my mom and the grandparents I've never met. This is my home for the next month and a half, whether I like it or not.

We pass through congested intersections filled with cars and motorcycles, trucks and donkey carts. I see squat buildings that are obviously offices, and tall glass structures that may or may not be offices. One is definitely a mall, and it rises to the sky. Soon, the streets broaden; the cars thin out. We must be in a different part of the city.

I squint at the street sign. Sunset Boulevard. Funny, Dad once sent me a postcard from Sunset Boulevard in California, a year after he left. It was the only time he ever sent me anything. Is this an omen? He's a journalist and travels a lot, so he could be anywhere in the world right now. Thanks to Google, I know he's traveled to lots of cool (and some hot) places. The last time I checked, about six months ago, he was the Asian correspondent of a fancy-pants newswire service somewhere in China. Still, I like to think of him in sunny California, surfing the waves and reporting on shark attacks.

I lean my face back against the window, taking in the big houses and the towering boundary walls with barbed wire on the top. This journey is never-ending.

I look sideways at Mom. She's breathing deeply from her mouth, a sure sign she's asleep. Her hands are folded neatly in her lap, fingers stained deep blue from the last painting she worked on before we left Houston. She can never get the stains out properly.

I rummage in my backpack and find my little square journal. It's got a gray leathery cover, and thick lined paper. My purple gel pen is tucked inside, serving as a bookmark.

Dear Dad,

You won't believe that I'm on a different continent from all my friends, right this minute. I'm awake while they're all sleeping, dreaming of who knows what. It's early morning here in Karachi, all the way in South Asia.

We're taking what Mom calls a long-overdue vacation. She's finally got a job at a private school as the art teacher, and we have the whole summer to celebrate instead of worrying about money as usual. My best friend, Zoe, is spending the summer in Italy. Isn't she L-U-C-K-Y? I would give my left arm to go to Europe.

Instead, I'm in Pakistan, which Mom says means "land of the pure." Ugh. It's pure, all right—pure haze, pure dust. Pure heat.

Have you ever been to Pakistan? Somehow I doubt it. A white man with light brown eyes and blond hair would really stand out here. Mom says this place will grow on me if I just give it a chance, but at the moment I'd give anything to be with you. Would you give anything to be with your family again?

Love,

Your daughter, Mimi

The taxi screeches to a stop in front of a sprawling white house with a balcony on the second floor and huge windows covered with metal bars. There are more *VOTE!* posters plastered on the boundary wall, along with colorful graffiti. "Is this it, ma'am?" the taxi driver calls out in Urdu.

Mom straightens up, yawning. I'm always amazed at her ability to take cat naps and wake up refreshed. I, on the other hand, wake up grouchy as a cat without whiskers. "Still the same," she says quietly, staring at the houses outside with a dreamy expression.

I scramble out of the car without being told and stretch on the street. "This is practically a mansion," I whisper in awe.

Mom joins me and grins. She's standing up straighter than I've seen in a long time. "Welcome to my childhood home, Mimi, my darling!" she says, and strides up to the gate to ring the bell.

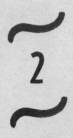

SAKINA
A LETTER WITH A HOPEFUL MESSAGE

"Hurry up, Sakina. Your father is leaving," Amma calls from the kitchen. I fold the letter carefully and stuff it into my little bag. The tiffin with Abba's lunch and mine is warm inside, and I want to make sure the letter doesn't get wet, or worse, destroyed. It's something called condensation, which makes hot things sweat like an old woman on a summer day.

Amma is squatting in the little courtyard of our home, washing clothes in the sink as the pipe sputters murky water into the big open trough. A pile of clothes lies in a heap at her feet, every single kameez my brother Jamshed has dirtied from the hours he plays outside. She looks up at me and frowns. "What took you so long, girl? Abba needs to be on time—you know that!"

"I was putting our food in the tiffin."

"Good." She utters a tired sigh and turns back to the sink. "Make sure your abba eats everything. He needs his strength to work."

This goes without saying, of course. Abba often forgets to eat, so it's my job to remind him. Sit with him and make him eat, if need be. Sometimes he's the father and I'm the child. Other times he's the child.

My brother is running about in the courtyard, pretending to be a bird. "Be a good boy today, Jammy," I tell him, and he grins at me.

Abba is waiting on his motorcycle, smiling despite the fact that we're very late. "I'm sorry, Abba," I huff, and climb on behind him, holding my bag between our two bodies.

"Tuck your dupatta in," he reminds me as he starts driving. "You don't want it to get stuck in the back wheel."

I know this already, but I check my dupatta anyway. Last year, a girl from our neighborhood died because her dupatta got tangled in the back wheel of the motorcycle she was riding, making her fall into oncoming traffic. "It's fine," I assure him, and we're off. Out of our narrow, cobbled street, past the election banners in bright colors. I wave goodbye to the milkman and the sweeper. I see a half-naked toddler investigating the rainwater drain with a stick and shout, "Wash your hands afterward!" He stares at me like I've said an alien thing.

Soon, we're cruising on the big road that leads toward the rich people's houses. The morning is already sweltering hot, but the wind rushes on my face and around my body like it's playing a game of hide-and-seek. I close my eyes and lean forward until my head touches Abba's back. He smells of soap and the mustard oil he smooths his shiny hair back with every morning. *My mother used to say it strengthens hair better than all those new shampoos on the market,* he always tells me. I don't like the smell of mustard oil, but I'd never tell Abba that.

We can't afford the fancy shampoos anyway, so I make do with soap and water—just a tiny bit, because we have to share one big bucket of water among us each day: Amma, Abba, and myself, plus four-year-old Jamshed. Water is more precious than the gold rich ladies buy from their air-conditioned malls with guards outside. Water is life. Gold is . . . colored rock.

I listen to the hum of the motorcycle engine, the roar of cars around us, the beep of horns as they pass us, telling us to hurry, hurry, hurry. Abba is probably going to be late, but he never shows an ounce of anger or worry on his face. That's what I love best about him. All our neighbors' parents fight in the evening, angry that the water is finished, or the electricity is gone again, or the gas isn't coming and they can't cook. Abba just lies back on his bed, no matter how hot it is, and murmurs, "It'll be all right. God will provide."

I'm not sure I believe that. God listens to rich people, not to people like Abba and me. Behind my closed eyelids, I can see the letter as if it's right in front of me.

Dear Sakina Ejaz:

We regret to inform you that you've failed the English portion of your admission test to New Haven School. Because of your high scores in science and mathematics, you are eligible for one more attempt at the English section on Friday, July 27, at 8:00 a.m. Please arrive early and check in at Gate 1. This letter will serve as your admission.

The letter is made up of huge words, but their meaning is clear. I failed the admission test because I'm not good enough. This isn't a total surprise, of course. I know only a little bit of English thanks to the cartoons I steal away to watch at Abba's place of work in between my chores. If Begum Sahiba ever knew I watched those cartoons, she'd be livid. Abba's warned me about slacking. We can't afford to be out of a job.

And I can't afford to fail this admission test one more time.

We reach Begum Sahiba's house at 10:00 a.m. sharp. Abba has managed to be on time even though we left fifteen minutes late. "See, God helps us in little things," he whispers to me as he checks his watch and slides his motorcycle into the driveway.

I make a face behind his back. God doesn't care if we are early or late, but I can't say that to him. It would break his heart.

The guard opens the gate and motions us inside. "The guests will be here soon," he urges. "You need to hurry and get to work. There's a lot to be done."

The guests. I've been hearing whispers from the servants all week long about the famous guests from America. Begum Sahiba's daughter, who I've never seen, is finally coming back to Pakistan with a child. More than that, I know nothing, nor do I care to. The other servants gossip about how the daughter married some white man and Begum Sahiba almost had a heart attack. They say the child is white. They say she's probably rude and ill-mannered. These rich people and their family issues seem so stupid to me. Six children died in my neighborhood last year because of heat stroke.

That's what I care about, making sure something like that doesn't happen to my family.

We hurry inside and get to work. Tahira, the maid who cleans the house and washes the clothes, is bustling about as if she's on an important mission. There are bedsheets to be changed, new towels to be placed carefully in all the bathrooms.

She pauses at the kitchen table to drink some water and rest. "Wonder what the Americans will bring for us," she says, grinning. Her front tooth is missing, and she annoys me with her constant chattering.

I shrug. "I don't think they'll bring anything for you," I tell her. She's older than me, possibly as old as Amma, or at least close. But she has no common sense.

"Why not?" she retorts. "Begum Sahiba's guests always give us some money when they leave."

"You're being greedy," I grumble, turning away to my tasks. "Just go do your job, otherwise Begum Sahiba is going to fire you. That's what she did to the last maid who spent too much time chatting."

A look of alarm crosses Tahira's face, and she leaves her water on the table to run out.

"You shouldn't have scared her, my dear," Abba tells me, but he's smiling. I smile back. He knows how much Tahira gets on my nerves.

I'm searching for an answer when he coughs slightly,

giving me a warning glance. The next second, Begum Sahiba glides into the kitchen. She's tall and very thin. She's wearing a light green silk sari with white peacocks on the border. Her hair is in a bun at the nape of her neck. "Ejaz," she says, and her voice cracks like a whip. "You're finally here! Why must you always be late?"

Abba hangs his head. I want to shout that we are right on time, but that's unthinkable. Servants have been dismissed for lesser sins. We both wash our hands at the sink—I marvel at the water running out of the tap in gushes—and get to work. I take out pots and pans from the cabinets under the stove and oil canisters from the pantry, and line up the spices. Abba is the head cook, and I'm his assistant. Still, it's Begum Sahiba who decides the menu.

We wait for today's orders. She's got a list as long as her bony, gold-bangled arm. Biryani. Shami kabab. Chicken karahi. And nuggets.

I'm guessing that last is for the American girl.

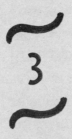

MIMI
THE MANSION AND ITS ROYALTY

I'm not sure what I'm expecting when the buzzer sounds sharply, and the gate swings open smooth as syrup. I peer inside, one hand holding my backpack tightly. The taxi driver has gone, leaving our luggage on the street under a scraggly tree.

We drag the suitcases inside, and the gate swings shut behind us with a clang that makes me jump. On my left is a big garden, with clipped grass and potted plants along the sides. A few white cane chairs are arranged on the far side, waiting to be sat on. I eye them, wondering if Mom ever sat on them, reading or just enjoying the breeze. Wondering everything about Mom right now. I never dreamed she grew up in a house like this.

Behind the gate stands a thin old man with white hair and a long white beard. "Samia Ji! Welcome!" he cries in Urdu, his face creasing into a smile.

Mom smiles, too, and nods. "Malik, I can't believe you're still here!" She turns to me. "Malik was my parents' driver since I was a little girl. He used to drive me everywhere. To school, then to college, and to my friends' houses. Everywhere!"

Malik is still smiling. "Everywhere," he echoes. "I'd have picked you up from the airport if I'd known the time."

Mom waves and continues toward the house. "Getting a taxi was no trouble at all. I'm just so happy to see you again!"

She's already walking up the long driveway to the house, a suitcase in her right hand, long strides as if she owns the place. Wait, does she? I pick up the second suitcase and follow quickly, not wanting to be left behind. Malik follows us, saying "Alhamdolillah" over and over. There are a few steps, and then a porch, and by the time we reach the front door with our things, the door opens by itself. I sneak a hand into Mom's, and she squeezes it in a way that makes me think that perhaps, unexpectedly, she's nervous as well.

A woman stands behind the door and motions us in. When she smiles I see a tooth missing. I'm ready to smile back and offer my standard Urdu greeting, meager as it is—*Salaam. Kya haal hai?*—but Mom walks inside without even glancing in her direction, so I bow my head and follow. Is that a relative? A servant? There are no answers to all the questions buzzing in my head like the pesky flies in the airport.

But there are no flies in here, only an echoing silence that feels claustrophobic. We walk through a hallway with marbled floors and faded tapestries on the walls, then through double doors into what looks like a highly formal living room. A cool air envelops me, making me groan with happiness. Air-conditioning, the chilly kind that comes from a unit, and not the central air in Houston.

I look around with interest. There are petite armchairs covered in lush red velvet, small round side tables with unusual items like a white chessboard and a collection of glass figurines. An elegant golden chandelier hangs from the middle of the ceiling. I feel my eyes rounding until they're stretched like golf balls, and my mouth is probably open, although I'm too shocked to care. Can this really be my mom's childhood house?

Mom is looking around as well, but with obvious distaste. "Flaunting their wealth as usual," she mutters as she flings our bags on the floor dangerously close to the table with the glass figurines. I want to shout, to ask why we've been living in a one-bedroom apartment in Houston for so many years if there was all . . . this . . . here, but she doesn't look like she's in a mood to talk just now. I gingerly put down my backpack and smooth my hair with my hands. Anyone living in this mansion is sure to be super elegant and not smelling like airports.

I step over our bags and walk around to the far side of the room. A small glass case contains beautifully dressed dolls standing in a variety of poses. They have such exquisite faces, and their clothes make them look like fashionistas. Or brides. I squat on the floor and press my face against the glass to stare at them.

"Samia! At last!" A movement makes me turn my head, and for a moment I think I'm staring at Mom's laptop screen during a late-night Skype session. A woman glides through the doors of the room as if she's the queen of the castle. Her graying hair is tied in a bun, and glasses dangle on her neck with a pearl string. Her green sari dazzles and shimmers. Behind her is a man in a crisp brown suit. I blink. Is there a party? I cross my arms over my poop emoji and smooth my hair again. I hope that smell isn't coming from me. When did I last take a shower? I can't remember.

"Ammi," Mom says, very politely. "Assalamu alaikum."

The lady reaches forward, and they hug. It's awkward

even from a distance, as if they're both made from prickly cactus. The man stands by, fidgeting. I bet his suit is too tight for him. It looks brand-new and totally uncomfortable. I suddenly have an urge to giggle, and I bite my lip. Call it intuition, but my grandmother doesn't look like she has a sense of humor.

"You're late," she says accusingly in perfect English. "You didn't get caught in one of those election processions, did you? They are crawling all over the city these days, drumming up votes, making lots of noise." She wrinkles her nose as if she can smell something stinky.

"Election? What election?" Mom straightens up and turns to her father. Their hug is less awkward, more genuine.

"We're going to elect our next prime minister in six weeks, my dear. It's all very exciting." He holds her at arms' length and smiles gently. "Thank God, you finally came to visit!"

"Well, you two wouldn't stop insisting," Mom answers dryly. "Plus your offer to pay for our tickets was . . . very generous."

"Nonsense. It was our pleasure!" He has a faraway look in his eyes. "How long has it been? Ten years?"

"Twelve," Mom corrects, and her voice is rough. She clears her throat and continues, "Mimi is eleven now, remember?"

"Where is Mimi, anyway?" my grandmother grunts, looking around.

I stand up and clear my throat. They all turn to me with startled eyes. "Maryam, darling!" The lady holds out her thin arms in an imperious command. Her voice is so fake, it's dripping sweet.

My feet refuse to move. Mom waves to me, making faces to tell me I'll get in trouble if I don't move immediately, into the open arms of the grandmother I haven't really known until now. Then the man walks over and envelops me in a hug. "Maryam, my dear, how big you've grown!" he says, smiling. "Your mother hardly ever sends us pictures of you."

"She doesn't sit still long enough to take pictures" is Mom's hasty reply, and I'm shocked because this is not exactly true. I spend hours in my room, reading. I stare at her, and she grins back sheepishly, acknowledging the lie.

I decide to forgive her. We're a team, she always says. I hug the man—his suit is super itchy—and smile at the lady. "Assalamu alaikum, Nana and Nani!" I say brightly, in my best Urdu accent.

She loses her saccharine smile. "Nani? I'm too young to be called Nani!"

Nana chuckles. "Well, this is your granddaughter right here, so that makes you a Nani, dear wife!"

She's not happy, I can tell. I bite my lip again to stop myself from laughing. She looks as if she's eaten a rotten egg. Mom's biting her lip, too, trying to keep still and serious. "Fine. Call me whatever you like," Nani grumbles, frowning darkly. She reaches out to a little golden bell on the table and rings it; the sound makes me jump a little. "Sakina, where are you?" she barks in Urdu. "Take these two to their rooms. They'll want to freshen up and change before lunch."

Nana gives me another hug. "I need to change too," he whispers with a wink. "This suit your nani forced me to wear to welcome you is as tight as a noose."

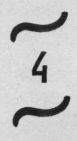

SAKINA
THE AMERICANS

I lead the guests upstairs to the second floor, where the bedrooms are. It's the first time since I started working here that these rooms have been used. Begum Sahiba and Sahib Ji sleep downstairs in a bedroom that's almost as big as my entire house. The upstairs is usually dark and empty, the curtains drawn tightly over the windows, the doors closed firmly.

Not anymore. The woman—Samia Ji—is rushing up the staircase with her arms wide open, her mouth stretched into a smile. "Oh, this place is still the same!" she gushes, pointing. "Here's my room, and that one right there was my brother's, and to the left was our library where we read books and did our homework!"

I try to imagine a room full of books, dedicated to

studying. In my house, there's one bedroom where my entire family huddles together at night, a verandah where Amma cooks and washes clothes while Jammy plays, and a little cupboard for a toilet. Oh, to have a room with a door I could close on the rest of the world and read. Maybe that would improve my English.

I look up and find the American girl watching me with eyes that are so light brown they seem almost transparent. Her hair is a lighter shade than mine, shoulder length and held back with a sparkly headband. She's tall, although Abba's told me she's my age. "American children grow taller and bigger," he once said. "They eat better food and have fewer worries than us Pakistani folk." I can't believe that this could be true. We eat and drink just fine, thank you very much.

"What's your name?" the American girl asks in English. We're at the top of the stairs, and her mother has disappeared into one of the bedrooms to investigate her childhood memories. We stand awkwardly together, me in my stained shalwar kameez, she in her T-shirt and jeans.

I freeze. People don't usually talk to me in Begum Sahiba's house. They just look right through me as if I don't even exist. Even Abba seems to forget I'm there until I accidentally drop a pan on the floor and he jerks around to give me a look of annoyance. When he's cooking, he likes to have complete silence in the kitchen.

"Um, Sakina," I answer, my voice low. I hope she's not going to start talking to me, because I can't speak too much English without making a fool of myself.

Too late. She opens her mouth and a string of words flow out like the Indus River: smooth on top, but rocky and dangerous underneath. Normally, I can understand English quite well, but her accent is strange. She opens her mouth too wide for *o* and *a* and softens her *t* for no reason. It's the accent I've heard on Sahib Ji's television when he watches movies in the afternoon. Movies filled with guns and buildings that blow up unexpectedly.

I focus on her mouth to try to understand her. ". . . short for Maryam."

I nod. "Salaam, Maryam."

She frowns. "No, call me Mimi. Nobody calls me Maryam. It's so . . ." and then I lose her. She's still talking when her mother walks up to us and snaps her fingers.

"Come on, Mimi, let's get settled in. You can talk to your new friend later."

They walk away toward the first bedroom, the one that used to be Samia Ji's childhood room. I watch them leave and shut the door firmly, my mouth open. *I'm not her friend*, I want to say, but there's nobody to hear me.

✳ ✳ ✳

At lunchtime, I set the table with Tahira's help. On normal weekday afternoons, there's hardly a dish or two on this table. Begum Sahiba and Sahib Ji eat in silence, sharing one meat dish and a side vegetable or daal with roti. Today is special, of course. All the food Abba and I have been cooking since morning is spread out like a king's feast. There are also bottles of mineral water and Coke and apple juice—the last probably for Mimi.

"Where's the roti?" Begum Sahiba snaps in Urdu.

I hasten back from the kitchen with fresh roti. "Here!" I say, hoping she's not angry. The last time roti was late to the table, she screamed like a banshee.

Mimi's mother takes one, then turns to me and smiles. "It's so light and fresh," she marvels. "Who made it?"

I blink at her. Why does she care who cooked the food? Her business is only in eating it. "I did," I finally admit.

"That's amazing! My daughter can't cook to save her life!" She casts a teasing look at Mimi, who sticks her tongue out at her mother.

The horror! I wait with a sick fascination for Mimi's mother to shout, or even smack her. Nothing. What sort of people are these Americans? Sticking your tongue out at an elder is the height of rudeness.

Begum Sahiba obviously thinks the same thing.

"Don't be rude, child," she tells Mimi with a frown.

Sahib Ji pats her hand. "Let them be, dear. It's only teasing. They don't consider it a big deal, and neither should you."

I can see an argument brewing. Careful not to meet Begum Sahiba's eye, I push the biryani toward Mimi's mother. "Here, try this. My abba made all this food."

Mimi's mother looks suitably impressed. "Did he?"

I nod proudly. "Yes, ma'am. He's been working here as the cook for almost five years."

"Okay, Sakina, no need to talk so much," Begum Sahiba interrupts. "Go check on the kitchen; start washing the dishes or something. Don't just go in and sit idly."

I grit my teeth. Abba and I haven't eaten yet. After a moment, I slink away, trying not to notice that Mimi is watching me.

"So," I hear Mimi's mom say as I leave, "tell me more about this election. Who are the candidates this year?"

In the kitchen, I find Abba putting the final touches on the kheer, the rice pudding the family will be served as dessert. He ladles it out in a shallow crystal bowl shaped like a flower and sprinkles sliced almonds and pistachios on top. "Abba, eat first," I tell him as I take out our tiffin from the cupboard. "They're talking politics. They won't ask for dessert for at least half an hour."

Abba is diabetic, so he can't eat most of the food he so lovingly cooks for the family. That's why I cook in the morning before we leave the house and bring our food with us. Abba's worked in houses where the owners allowed him to cook and eat in their kitchen, but Begum Sahiba is a dragon, and a selfish one at that. She wants not a grain of rice or a sprinkle of flour to go to any of her servants. She keeps count of everything in the pantry, in the storeroom, in the attic, and in the garage outside.

So I prefer our own way. Who needs to be beholden to a rich woman, anyway? I keep a little bag of our own things in the cabinet under the sink: a sack of flour, some oil, and a bag of sunflower seeds for afternoon snacking.

Today I've made spinach curry with a few pieces of turnip. I'm nowhere as good a cook as Abba, but I'm learning. There are two extra roti I cooked a few minutes ago, still steaming hot. We sit on the kitchen floor and eat, father and daughter, as we've been doing for years. He smiles at me as he eats. "Delicious as usual," he says, even though I'm not the best cook. Still, we are together, and that is enough to make me smile back.

MIMI
MOVE SOME CHESS PIECES ON THE BOARD

I'm woken by the sound of quarreling outside my open balcony. At first I think I'm back in my apartment, where the next door neighbor Mrs. Peabody always shouts at her grandson to eat his breakfast. *You're so skinny, you're going to fall down from exhaustion one day! Eat some eggs and bacon, for God's sake!* The grandson is twenty–something and works downtown. I find it hilarious to imagine ancient Mrs. Peabody trying to jam bacon and eggs down his throat as he gets ready to go to work.

I snuggle in my bed, listening, slowly realizing that things are not the same. The feel of the fabric over me is different—less scratchy than in Houston, fluffier and more luxurious. There are crows outside, cawing in angry tones. My street in Houston has nothing but little robins and sparrows, tweeting happy little good mornings to each other. The quarreling is also different. Mrs. Peabody never sounded so . . . furious.

Then it strikes me. I'm in Pakistan, far away from robins and sparrows and cranky old Mrs. Peabody.

I struggle to sit up, my eyes only half open. The clock on the wall says 11:05 a.m., but I'm pretty sure that's not accurate. I feel like there's a ton of bricks on my head, like it's the middle of the night and I just can't wake up.

I drag myself out of bed and to the balcony with bare feet, rubbing my eyes at the brightness of the sun. Nani is standing on the ground below with her hands on her hips, screaming. "You killed all my rose bushes, you ulloo-ka-patha! Do you know how expensive they were? I got imported soil for them. I got special food for them. What is wrong with you?"

A man stands in front of her, hanging his head, wringing his hands. "Sorry, Begum Sahiba, please forgive me," he pleads in Urdu. "I'll be more careful next time."

This is better than a movie! I watch in fascination as Nani scolds the poor gardener for the next twenty minutes, wondering what *ulloo-ka-patha* means. She's wearing some sort of long sky-blue dress, but from my angle I can't tell if it's a sari or a nightgown. Her stick-thin arms are clad with the same gold bangles I saw yesterday. Does she sleep in them? Does she bathe in them and take them to the bathroom with her? I cover my mouth with my hand to stifle my giggles.

Nani's voice is loud enough to disturb the birds in the trees outside. I can't believe this is Mom's mother. Mom never screams at me, even that time a couple of years ago when I was practicing dance moves in her room and crashed into her worktable, spilling her paints on a half-finished painting. I still remember her face: horror, anger, and a twinge of panic. But she just led me out of the room and told me to practice dancing somewhere else. I didn't know until much later that she'd been commissioned by a famous Houston tycoon to paint that portrait.

I didn't know much about anything until recently. Like the fact that Mom's job at the Art Institute wasn't enough to pay the bills, and she used to try to sell her artwork to make a little money on the side. Or the fact that important people once paid her to paint their dogs' pictures in a series called Rich Pups that was later displayed in an art museum. She took me to the opening as a surprise earlier this year, not telling me she was the artist until people started coming up to congratulate her. "What elegance, what style!" a woman in a floor-length gown gushed. "Thank you for making my darling Boris look so . . . human!"

Mom was embarrassed. I could tell by her red cheeks and nervous smile. "I want to be known for my water-colors of nature, for my collages and my abstracts," she complained on the way home. "Painting dogs is so humiliating."

I didn't really understand. "Dogs are awesome," I told her dreamily. I'd been begging for a pet forever, but she said we couldn't afford it.

"It's not dogs, really." She gave a frustrated sigh and gazed out the windshield. "It's just the idea of a trivial topic like rich people's pets. All the classical artists became famous for landscapes and human portraits. Not animals. Especially not animals belonging to some pretentious old people who live in big mansions cut off from real people."

I didn't really understand what the big deal was then, but now watching Nani scream about her precious roses with their special food and seeing the poor gardener's shoulders slump dries up all my giggles like the bushes below me. Are Nani and Nana also pretentious old people who live in big mansions? And if so, what does that make me?

Dear Dad,

Do you ever get angry? Not annoyed or irritated, like most people, but a deep angry that makes you throw something at the wall and watch it crack. I know I'm not supposed to talk like that. I'm supposed to be a grateful girl who has all of life's blessings.

Sometimes I don't feel like that. Mom says several weeks in Pakistan will give me perspective and a new sense of gratitude. Doesn't that sound just like her? Everything she says is so neat and tidy, as if she's read it in a magazine. She does read lots of magazines, though!

I wonder what you like to read. I found a few Spider-Man comics in an old box under Mom's bed recently. Mom just snatched them from me and threw them in the trash, so I'm guessing they must have been yours. Or maybe she was just worried they were dirty from being under the bed for so long. Doesn't matter. I like to imagine you sitting in an armchair reading a Spider-Man comic book.

I much prefer Wonder Woman myself.

Until next time,

Mimi

In the afternoon, after a huge lunch and a short nap, Nana calls me to the TV room to sit with him. I've changed into black capri pants and a lime-green T-shirt with a slice of cake and the words *I EAT CAKE BECAUSE IT'S SOMEONE'S BIRTHDAY SOMEWHERE* on it. Mom is already there at a rickety wooden easel in the corner, testing some paints. "Where did all this come from?" I ask, amazed at how quickly she's created a space for herself in this house. Then I have to remind myself that this is Mom's house; she lived it in forever and ever. Before America. Before Dad and me.

Sure enough, she replies, "I found these old things in the closet in my bedroom," and a peaceful little smile creeps onto her face, making her look beautiful.

"This mother of yours used to be always painting, always painting," Nana tells me cheerfully. He's setting up a small wooden table in front of his armchair. "One time she even won a competition at school. Do you remember, eh, Samia darling?"

I sit down next to him, intrigued. Mom is bent over her easel, her hair falling onto her face, acting as if she can't hear us. "How old was she?" I ask.

Nana takes out a slim rectangular black box from a drawer and opens it. It's a chess set. He begins to carefully set up the pieces, talking as he works. "She must have been your age, I think. And do you know what her prize was?"

I rack my brain. "A paint set?"

He looks up at me sharply. "Did she already tell you this story?"

I have to laugh at his aggravated expression. "I guessed. We have an art competition in my school every year, and the winner always gets something art-related. Like paints or a gift card to a craft store."

"And do you ever win, like your mother?"

I look over at Mom again. She's painting a face, but it's too soon to tell whose. She always takes the longest to complete faces, sometimes days or even weeks. I shrug. "Nah. Mom's the artist in the family, not me."

"Are you sure? Maybe you just never tried." He gestures to me to move a chess piece. Apparently we are going to play a game of chess, whether I like it or not. I move a pawn two spaces forward.

"Classic rookie move," he tells me with relish, and moves a knight. I stare at the board, trying to remember what I know about the game. Almost nothing. I move pieces randomly until Nana shouts with laughter and says, "Did nobody teach you to play chess, little girl?"

I shake my head. "Mom's too busy painting all the time, as you can see." I push out my lip and pretend to sob.

He shakes his head and laughs some more. "Well, then, consider this your education." He sets up the pieces again. "I'll go easy this time."

Mom shakes her paintbrush at me. "Serves you right for complaining about your mother!" But she gives me one of her little smiles, all warm and cheeky. Besides, I don't really mind playing chess with Nana. It doesn't seem so bad.

Halfway through the third game, a loudspeaker crackles to life, and a melodious sound fills the air around us. *Allahu akbar. Allahu akbar.* God is great. God is great. "What is that?" I ask Nana, looking around me for the source.

He waves his hand. "Oh, it's just the azaan from the mosque down the street. Very loud, I know, but it can't be helped. You'll get used to it in a few days."

"Azaan?" I know this word, although it's a hazy memory in my mind of visiting a mosque in Houston a long time ago, watching the worshippers prostrate themselves in a steady line in front of me.

"The call to prayer. The mosque puts it on the loudspeaker five times a day, every day." Nana adds, "In Urdu, we say *azaan*. The Arabic word for it is *adhaan*."

I decide I like *azaan* better. The word flows smoother, like caramel over ice cream. Mom closes her eyes and leans back against her chair, breathing deeply as if she's listening to some long-ago song from her childhood. I gaze at the chess pieces, letting the azaan wash over me like a soothing balm. It reaches deep into me and pings my chest.

When the azaan ends, the servant girl enters, bringing tea and a plateful of cookies in the shape of hearts, with red jam centers. I lean back and smile at her, but she gives me a serious look and turns away. Rude!

"Take some chai to Begum Sahiba in her room," Nana says, but kindly. He's nice to the servants, unlike Nani. I think of her shouting at the man about her roses. Nana doesn't look like he's ever shouted in his life. I wonder how the two of them get along.

I pick up a heart-shaped cookie and take a bite. Warm and soft, with a hint of sweetness. I munch, wiping crumbs away from my mouth. The servant girl leaves without a word, closing the door after her with a hard click.

6

SAKINA
A LITTLE HAVEN

Amma's been having her headaches again, so I spend Sunday morning doing all her chores instead of relaxing on my only day off from Begum Sahiba's house. Jammy has to be bathed, which is exhausting. I have to keep shouting at him to stop wasting water and settle down. He giggles and splashes me. Oof!

Abba relaxes on the charpai in the verandah, listening to the news on his ancient radio. Elections are coming up in six weeks, and the local candidates spend Sunday mornings debating each other. It sounds more like arguing, but I hardly listen anyway. What has any elected official ever done for poor people? Our neighborhood still doesn't have even one fully paved road, and the trash piles keep getting bigger and smellier.

The mosquitoes continue to bite us all, making us sick with malaria and Dengue fever.

"Everyone should refuse to vote for these people until they fulfill their promises from the last year," I grumble as I wash the floor with leftover bath water. The suds make the stone sparkle and shine, and for a minute I'm pleased, even though I know the heat will dry it all up before I'm finished cleaning.

"If only our neighbors were as clever as my daughter," Abba says affectionately. I roll my eyes, making sure he doesn't see. He's always telling everyone about how smart I am, how hardworking. It's embarrassing, but it also warms my heart in a way that few other things do.

I hum a little tune as I work. I'm not sure what it is, but the American girl in Begum Sahiba's house was listening to an English song all day yesterday, and now it's echoing in my head. All I could understand was *shake it shake it*, the rest was a shrill jumble of musical gibberish. She's got a small laptop on which she types messages, but she also likes reading books and writing in a little gray book. She keeps smiling at me, and I keep staring back, not knowing how to respond.

I finish up the cleaning, wash the dishes from the night before, then begin cooking lunch. It's the usual Sunday fare: spicy yellow daal, plain white rice, and roasted whole wheat roti. Abba will eat only the daal and roti, leaving the rice for everyone else.

At least that's what I'll make him do. He keeps "forgetting" that rice isn't good for his diabetes. He'll sneak some onto his plate when I'm not looking, and then I won't have the heart to make him put it back. "Just a few bites?" he'll wheedle, his eyes sparkling, his hand out like the beggars I see on the street, and I'll give in.

Later, when everyone is taking their daily afternoon nap, I crawl into my secret reading space. It's a tiny half room right behind the toilet, big enough for me to sit with my knees drawn up. Amma used it as a pantry a long time ago, storing dry items such as flour and sugar, but it's been years since we had enough money to buy extra. Nowadays, we make do with whatever we can buy, storing it all on a broad wooden shelf over the stove. This little space is now mine. I'd give anything to have a door at its entrance, so I could close it from the peeping eyes and greedy fingers of my little brother. But I have to be satisfied with a long swathe of jute fabric hung from the top of the entryway.

This room is my haven, my retreat, my paradise. It's almost completely empty of decoration, except a naked lightbulb on the ceiling, and one shelf on the side with a pile of books Abba's managed to scrounge from the houses where he's worked. They are torn hand-me-downs, one dug out from a garbage heap, a few yellowed from age. There's *My First Book of Animals*, a class-two textbook for science, and a mystery story about a girl named Nancy Drew, which has a ton of big words. There's a cookbook from 1978 with a woman in a checked red-and-white apron on the worn-out cover. Her hair is fine yellow like the silk I see in fabric stores in the market. She wears the sort of clothes I could never afford in a million years.

On the far corner of the shelf, hidden behind the books, is an old tin box. I don't need to open it to know what's inside. A sparkly black hair clip that belonged to Amma. A pretty brooch with a bright green gem I found on the street near Begum Sahiba's house last year. A bookmark with the words *Readers Are Leaders*. All my saved-up money, which is 243 rupees right now. And the letter from New Haven School. *Dear Sakina Ejaz* . . .

I push the tin can out of my mind. What really matters is that in this little room, cramped and uncomfortable, I can be the opposite of Sakina. I can dream of going to school, of learning all sorts of things from the earth to the stars. I can dream of being somebody else, not a cook's assistant at a mean old lady's house. Not a daughter with a checklist of chores and an ailing parent.

Not Sakina. Somebody else.

Amma always tells me to stop dreaming. She doesn't like it when I crawl into my little room to read. *You'll ruin your eyes, and then how will you work?* she often scolds me. *We need your extra income to survive—you know that.*

Yes, Amma, I know. I just close my eyes and pretend I can't hear her. Abba tells her to stop scolding me, that everybody needs a little space to dream once in a while. He's a softie. It was he who gave in and finally took me for the admission test to New Haven School last winter, after I kept pestering him every single day. *Just to see how smart I am, Abba, please?* I kept begging. So he relented, like I knew he would. He doesn't know I'm serious about going to school, about spending the whole day studying rather than earning money. He doesn't know how hard I've been practicing my subjects, spending hours at night reading after everyone is asleep. He thinks it's a phase I'll grow out of, so he humors me.

I shift and squirm, trying to find a comfortable space. I'm practicing math problems in a lined notebook I bought from the corner shop, but my legs are getting numb. Better to wait until evening. Sometimes at night after dinner, Abba sits with me and gives me sums to work on: What's fifty times eight, and what's three hundred divided by nine? Those are easy, almost too easy for me, but I don't tell him that. He only studied to class three when he was a child, before his father—my grandfather—died of tuberculosis and Abba had to work in his uncle's street café to support the family.

It's all right, though. I've realized that I can work on multiplication, division, and even fractions every single day when I measure ingredients for Abba in Begum Sahiba's kitchen, or buy vegetables from the man who brings the vegetable cart around every morning. I practice chemistry when I bake cakes and cook curries, and biology when I feed Sahib Ji's birds in the garden cages. He's got peacocks and pigeons and mynah birds, and each has a different diet. I watch everyone and everything around me, listen to early-morning children's shows on the radio, and eavesdrop when I walk past the school in my neighborhood.

The only thing I can't seem to master is speaking English. I know what it is: I need someone to speak to, someone who'll correct me when I'm wrong, tell me what to say and how to say it. I may be able to teach myself the basics, but if I'm to pass the admission test, I need a teacher.

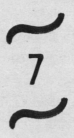

MIMI
MY FRUIT IS BETTER THAN YOURS

The servant girl is chopping a vegetable of some sort in the breakfast area when I go downstairs to get a drink of water. I think it's a squash, but I can't be sure. Everything is different in Pakistan. The cantaloupe I ate last night for dessert was white, instead of the melon orange I'm used to, and the taste was almost tart. The peaches are tiny; the bananas look like smaller, softer, blacker versions of ours.

So far, America 1, Pakistan 0. Unsurprising.

The kitchen is big and airy, with windows on the back wall showing glimpses of the garden. Two stoves are lit, each with a pot of something boiling, contributing to the humid air. The servant girl—her name is on the tip of my tongue—has a long braid tied with a yellow ribbon at the end. She's wearing a faded pink shalwar kameez with sleeves rolled up in a way that make it obvious her clothes originally belonged to someone else. She's tied her dupatta around her waist like she's about to wrestle.

"Good morning," I offer in English, before I remember that she speaks Urdu. Grr!

"Assalamu alaikum," she says at the same time. I want to shout *jinx!* but I doubt she'll understand. She couldn't catch most of what I was saying the first morning we got here.

I walk to the fridge and open it. I hardly ate any lunch; even the chicken nuggets were spicy. It's only our fourth day in Pakistan, and I'm sweating tiny streams from my forehead. Mom says I'll get used to the heat in no time, if only I leave my air-conditioned bedroom.

No, thank you. I'd rather get used to the little boxy air conditioner under my window that blasts icy air onto my face when I stand in front of it.

Right next door to my bedroom is Mom's, the one she used to sleep in when she was my age. She's shown me every corner of that room with excitement: the wall where she pinned posters of a boy band called Junoon, the closet drawer where she stashed all her cassettes of Indian movie songs, the balcony she used to sit on reading romance novels in the afternoon while her parents napped. Ew to the last one! I can't get over how rich she used to be.

Not anymore, though. In Houston, with me, she's just . . . average. Getting by. "Starving artist," she sometimes says jokingly. What a change that must be. Does she secretly hate her life? Does she wish she was a rich Pakistani again? Is that why we're really here?

I peer into the fridge as if it holds the answers to all my questions. "Do you need something?" the servant girl asks from behind me. Sakina, that's her name.

"Um, Coke?" I turn around and mutter, trying to keep my words to a minimum to avoid making a mistake in Urdu. Then I smile, hoping she'll help me.

Sakina sighs noisily and stands up, raking her chair on the tiled floor. She walks to the open fridge and points. "In the last shelf," she tells me very slowly in Urdu, as if I'm some stupid kid who can't see properly. I look at where she's pointing. Oh. The Coke cans are right there in the front.

I take one and go back to the kitchen table. "Can I sit here?" I ask hesitantly. I'm pretty sure I said that correctly, no grammatical mistakes or anything.

She frowns. "Why are you asking me? I'm just a servant. This whole house belongs to your nani, so you can sit wherever you like."

I understand that loud and clear. Wow, she's mad

about something. I almost run back out of the kitchen, but I need some privacy, and this is the only place nobody will look for me. A few hours ago, Mom even barged into the bathroom while I was doing my business, demanding to know if I had diarrhea. I screamed.

"Listen"—I try to smile—"where I come from, we don't have servants. Or at least my family doesn't. My friend Zoe has a . . . um . . . cleaning lady that comes in once a week, but that's not me."

I'm so proud of having said all that in Urdu. I smile at her, but all I get in return is a stare. She doesn't care. I sit on the chair farthest from her and take out my journal from under my arm. I ignore Sakina and begin to write.

Dear Dad,

Summer vacations are boring, if you know what I mean. Or maybe you don't because you're an adult. You must be super busy with work and everything. Do you ever take a break? Where do you go?

Pakistan is continuing to get on my nerves. There are flies everywhere, and last night a bug crawled into my bed. I woke up with red, itchy spots on my arms and legs. DISGUSTING AND CREEPY!

Mom is being super strange here. She and Nani (another word for grandmother, in case your Urdu is even worse than mine) hardly ever talk, but they have these tight little conversations about nothing that seem to have all this unspoken history behind them. Like that one time you visited us in our Houston apartment when I was six . . . remember that? It's the only time I ever saw you after you left, and you and Mom sat on opposite ends of the couch and said all these little nothings. Isn't the weather nice today? Did you watch the new Star Wars *movie yet? And then Mom said, "How do you think I'd have time to watch movies when I'm taking care of a child single-handedly?"*

Anyway, Mom and Nani have the same weird little conversations. Funny how one reminded me of the other. Ha!

Nana, aka Grandfather, is awesome, though. He tells the corniest jokes, and he's got a huge collection of old books that I can't wait to look through. Most of them seem to be about engineering, but he says there are a few coffee-table books with pictures and maps. Although I'm not sure why those books are stuffed in the back of a bookshelf. Shouldn't they be on a coffee table? Ha, ha!

Nana's also teaching me to play chess. I know quite a bit already. Do you know how to play chess? Don't worry if you don't—I can teach you when we meet.

*If we meet. As they say in Pakistan, land of the flies,
inshallah.*

    Your loving daughter,
    Mimi xoxoxo

A noise startles me. I look up to see Sakina staring
at me intensely. She clears her throat. "What are you
doing?" she asks, pointing her knife toward my journal.

I put my hands over the page. "Nothing," I reply.
Then I reconsider. It's not like she can read English
or anything. "It's a notebook my mom gave me. I'm
supposed to write down all the places I visit and new
things I experience."

"Like what?"

"Um . . ." I look around. "Like, take those bananas.
They are so different from the ones I eat in the US, so
they'd be a new experience I could write about. How
they're . . . um . . . mushy and gooey on the inside and
brownish on the outside."

She sits up straight and squares her shoulders. "Our
bananas are the best. They come straight from the
farms, no pesticides." At least that's what I think she
says. I don't really know the Urdu word for farms. Or
pesticides.

I find myself wanting to smile, but I don't. There's
something about her that makes me want to rile her up,

get a response. She's so determined, with her mouth set in a straight line and her scowl ready to display itself at a moment's notice. I say with complete seriousness, "No offense, but our fruits are so much better than yours. Everything I've eaten here so far tastes . . . unusual." I turn my lips downward to show her what I mean. Strange, possibly yucky. Nothing to write home about.

She looks at me with her mouth open. The scowl is gone, replaced by a smoothness that makes her seem almost at ease. There is a sudden, unexpected gleam in her eye. She puts down her knife and gets up deliberately. She goes to the fridge and comes back with a yellow oval fruit. "I have . . . challenge for you," she says.

And guess what? She says the sentence in clearly spoken English.

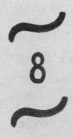

8

SAKINA
A DEAL WITH THE DEVIL

The American girl watches as I slice the mango. Juice drips down my fingers, but I resist the urge to lick them. Mangoes are the king of all the fruit, the pride of Pakistan, but they're so expensive Abba can hardly afford them. Begum Sahiba allows the servants to eat the older ones from the back of the fridge, those that are almost rotting. I don't care; I'd eat a rotten mango over an American banana any day.

This mango is definitely not rotten. It's fat and juicy, just arrived from the market in a box filled with about twenty-five others. "Only for the guests," Begum Sahiba had warned us with a glare. Of course. I wasn't going to have Abba lose his job over a mango.

But now, I have an idea. It didn't occur to me until

I saw Mimi write in her little gray book. Maybe these guests will be a blessing after all, just like Amma says. *Guests always come with blessings from God,* she says. I've never really agreed with her. Whenever we have guests at our house—cousins, aunts and uncles, long-lost friends come to Karachi from the villages to see the sights—they seem to bring with them empty stomachs, unwashed clothes, and unshakeable thirst. Amma has to cook more, Abba has to go the big market and bring home plastic bags filled with meat and vegetables, and I have to wash clothes all day long. Guests are nothing but work.

But this American girl, with all her high-and-mighty ways, may just be worth all the work I do for her. She's very interesting in some ways. Her clothes, for instance, always have words on them. I've never seen girls wear clothes with sentences written on them, only boys. Maybe this is how they do things in America. Today, her shirt is light blue. On one side is a tomato with stick legs and a mustache; on the other side is a ketchup bottle. On top of the tomato is a speech bubble with the words *BRO, IS THAT YOU?*

I think they call ketchup *bro* in America. How strange.

I set the mango in front of her, gleaming gold. I've cut it into strips the traditional way: two big sections down the lengths, and one big pit. She stares at it uncertainly. "I've only ever seen mango cut into cubes, and they're usually orange."

I try not to shudder. She's ignorant and slightly dumb. Still, the fact that she knows English is enough to increase her value in my eyes. I stretch my lips into what I hope is a smile. "Try. Promise you like."

She turns to me. "That's another thing. How do you know English?"

I have to be patient, I tell myself. "Do you think I'm . . . what do you say . . . uneducated?" I ask her, but gently. There's a high chance she actually does think all Pakistanis are uneducated. Yesterday, she marveled at a McDonald's ad on television. I wonder what she'll say when she hears we also have Pizza Hut, Hardee's, KFC, and all the other American restaurant chains. Not to mention the latest iPhones. Her eyes will probably pop out of their sockets.

She shrugs. "I don't know. You work here all day. When do you go to school?"

I squelch my frustration. Her questions are too many, too fast. I'd rather she taste the mango. I gesture toward it. "First eat. Then I answer."

The kitchen door bangs open, and we both look up, startled. Tahira bustles in, holding a laundry basket full of wet clothes. "Salaam, Maryam Ji." She grins, bobbing her head. "Eating delicious mangoes, I see?"

Mimi looks at her uncertainly. "Is it any good, do you think?" She uses the wrong word for good, which makes me relax just a bit. This girl isn't perfect either.

Tahira stares at her with round eyes. "Any good? What sort of question is that? A mango is the best fruit, the sweetest, the juiciest! When I was a young girl, my friends and I would climb up the tree in our village and eat two or three at a time. Once my brother got a stomachache so bad—"

This could go on forever. "Don't you have to hang those clothes outside, Tahira?" I prompt, giving her a hard look.

Grumbling under her breath, she departs out the back door to the clothesline.

"Now, where were we?" I say, shutting the door firmly behind her.

Mimi looks at the door, then back at her plate doubtfully. She picks up one slice gingerly and bites into it. I look at her face as it transforms from boredom to interest, and finally to utter delight. She gobbles down the slice, then another, then sucks on the pit. Juice dribbles down her chin, but she continues to eat.

"Wow, wow, wow!" she whispers. "What on earth is this fruit? How is it so amazing?"

"So you agree? Pakistan wins?"

She licks her lips and reaches for another mango

slice. "Oh yeah, definitely. Pakistan ten, America zero."

I'm pretty sure that's a sports comparison. Americans are known to be very sporty. I sit down next to her and point to her journal. "So now you make deal with me?"

She nods eagerly. "Anything. I'm dying to hear all about it."

I consider this. I know she's not really dying, so her excited expression must mean she's extremely eager. "Why?" I ask.

"Are you kidding? You're finally talking to me. Do you know how many times I've tried making friends with you, but you just scowl and walk away? I mean, you're the only person my age in a thousand-mile radius. Why wouldn't I want to talk to you and hear about how your English is so good but you work as a cook? It's fascinating!"

I can feel the scowl she's talking about worry my forehead. Despite her lightning-fast speech, I've managed to get the gist of it. How easy her life is, how simple.

I struggle to explain the facts of life to her. "I'm a servant. Your nani would . . . kill me? . . . if she see me sitting around, eh, chatting."

She immediately looks around the kitchen. "I think she's sleeping," she whispers. Interestingly, she seems as afraid of Begum Sahiba as everyone else.

"Of course she is sleeping," I say. "Everyone sleeps in the afternoon."

"The lunch your father made was very good. My mom says she needs a nap after such delicious food."

I nod. Anyone who praises my abba can't be all bad. "Thank you. He work very hard."

"Works very hard."

I pause. "What?"

"Works very hard, not work . . ." She stops and bites her lip. "Never mind. Where is your abba right now?"

I wave to the back door. "There is a little covered . . . eh . . . outside where all the servants lie down to . . . eh . . . relax in afternoon. I don't like to sit with them because, you know, the driver, he smoke, and it make my eyes water."

She nods. "I hate cigarette smoke too. It's so yucky."

Yucky. I like this word. But I don't tell her that. I have to ask her about the deal before it's too late.

"So," I say, switching to Urdu, but speaking slowly so she can understand me. "You asked me how I know English. My abba used to work in a different house when I was little. My job was to play with the children of the family. The children had a tutor who came to teach them math and science and English. I was there the whole day, every day, and so I learned with them. Writing in English, just a little bit. But I can read a lot.

The newspaper, storybooks, the signs on the street. They didn't even realize it."

She is silent. "So you never actually went to school?" She speaks in Urdu too, broken and hesitant.

I take a deep breath. There's no use getting angry. It's a reality I can't escape. "Poor people have to work. We don't have the luxury of school."

"I . . . I . . ." She switches to English. "I'm so sorry."

I blink away the fierceness from my eyes. This is good, I remind myself. She's feeling sorry for me, which means she may help me. "I'll be okay now you are here," I tell her firmly. "You can teach me English."

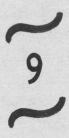

MIMI
IF PIGS COULD FLY, WHERE WOULD THEY FLY TO?

Sakina's words echo in my head all night. *Teach me how to speak English so I can pass the admission test for school.* Her English isn't all bad. She knows words, but not grammar and tenses. Probably the same as my Urdu. I agreed without a single thought, of course, right there in the kitchen while the family and servants all took their afternoon nap. How could I not? A deal is a deal, and that mango she fed me was truly delicious.

A cool breeze wafts in from my open window and makes the white cotton curtains billow in waves. My bed is on the other side of the room, a strong brown wooden thing with four huge posters and a leather headboard. It belonged to my uncle Faizan, who's studying to be a doctor in England. He and Mom are

Facebook friends, but he hardly ever calls on the phone because Mom says he's something called a millennial. Two years ago, he visited us in Houston during spring break. Mom took him around to see all the sights, and in the evenings they sat in our little living room and ate Pakistani takeout food from Kabob Kitchen down the street, keeping me company as I watched Nickelodeon. All I remember about that trip is that every sentence Mom and Uncle Faizan spoke started with *Do you remember . . . ?*

I lie back, staring at the sliver of moon, wondering if Sakina can see it from her bedroom too. What is her room like? Her house? Does she have brothers and sisters? A mom? I know nothing about her, except that she's always working, even in the afternoon when the others are sleeping. She goes home on the back of her father's motorcycle in the evening, her scarf fixed on her head, not even turning once to look at me.

I feel like the new girl in school, wanting the popular girl to like me. Only this isn't school, and the popular girl hasn't even seen the inside of one. There's a tightness in my chest at the thought of all the servants in Pakistan never going to school. All the poor children sitting on street corners and cleaning rich people's houses.

Nana's driver, Malik, took me and Mom for a drive around the neighborhood on our first day in Karachi.

We drove to a little park at the end of the street, and then to the Dunkin' Donuts around the corner. At the traffic light was a little boy around six or seven. His face was dusty and his clothes were torn. He held out a filthy hand and muttered words I couldn't catch because the window was rolled up and the music was blasting in our air-conditioned car.

I didn't sleep that night either.

I slowly sit up and take out my journal from the bedside table drawer. I know it's silly to write to a father who left me, who doesn't ever call or visit me. There's not even a small chance that he'll ever read the journal, but maybe that's why I like writing in it. I can say whatever is in my heart, ask a thousand questions, without any fear of being laughed at.

> *Dear Dad,*
>
> *Today I tried a new fruit: mango. I know it's not really new, but the taste of the Pakistani mango is so much better than anything I've ever eaten. I tried one, then another, and then a third, until my stomach was about to burst. My T-shirt has splotches of yellow on it, which I'm not sure can be washed off, but my heart is happy.*
>
> *I think I've made a friend. Her name is Sakina, and her biggest talent is cooking. Even the chicken nuggets*

she cooks are so soft and delicious, even though they're spicy. She's always so serious and sad, as if her entire body hurts. I'm going to see if I can make her smile. I bet she's got the prettiest smile.

By the way, do you wonder why I like nuggets so much? I still remember that day you took me to Chesterton for lunch. I was only five, so I don't really remember it, but I have the picture Mom took of us. Me in my white polka-dot dress and a bow in my hair, and you with that black T-shirt that said I DON'T LIKE MORNING PEOPLE. OR MORNINGS. OR PEOPLE.

I'm not really a morning person either. Did you know that?

Probably not.

Miss you,

Mimi

There's a little bit of a lie in what I've written. I do remember some things about that day. Snatches of fragrances. The tone of voices. Dad insisting that Mom take lots of pictures. Mom's annoyed face. Dad's aftershave lotion tickling my nose as he hugged me for the last time. I still remember that aftershave: musky fresh with a hint of lemon.

When I was younger, I used to think that smell was

the way all fathers smelled. Warm and lemony. I didn't know it was aftershave until one day in first grade I went to the mall with Mom. We passed by a perfume counter at Macy's and there, mingled with all the smells, was Dad's. "He's here!" I cried, jumping up and down right there in the Macy's cosmetics department. It took Mom about two seconds to realize what I meant, and why I thought Dad was around somewhere. She crouched down to meet me at eye level, gripping my hand hard enough to make me stop jumping. She closed her eyes for a second, and when she opened them, they were wet. "I'm sorry, sweetheart, it's not him," she whispered, her cheek close to mine. "It's the cologne he used to wear. Look."

She pointed to the counter. A bottle stood out from the rest, like a glass jar of betrayal. Terre d'Hermès.

In Uncle Faizan's bedroom at night, my eyes are suddenly heavy with tears.

There's a knock on the door, and I scramble to put away my journal. "Come in," I call out, even though I know it's Mom. She's the only person who knocks in threes. *Knock-knock*, then a pause, and then a *KNOCK*.

"Hey, I saw the light on under your door," she says as she enters. "It's almost midnight; why aren't you asleep?"

"I could ask you the same thing."

She sits on my bed, pushing my legs out of the

way. She's in her usual bedtime attire: striped pajama bottoms from Victoria's Secret, and a worn-out white cotton T-shirt with a big red heart in the center. "I was reading."

"I was writing," I reply without thinking.

"What were you writing?"

"In . . . in my journal," I stammer. "But you can't see. It's private."

She smiles and winks. "I understand perfectly." She sits back and rubs a hand over the bedspread. "You know, when I was little, I'd sneak into this room in the middle of the night to check up on your uncle. Sometimes we'd play cards together. Or Monopoly."

I make a face because I hate Monopoly. It's the longest and most boring game in the history of games. "I wish I had a brother," I say, although I don't really, at least not most of the time.

She frowns prettily. "No, you don't. Faizan used to drive me bonkers. Always getting into my paint supplies, teasing me about the smallest things. It was brutal."

I look closer at her. She has to be joking. Is she? I can't tell. "Yeah, but family is everything, right?" I say, quoting a slogan for an English-language commercial I saw on Nana's television the night before.

She rolls her eyes like a child. "Not my family. Or haven't you noticed?"

I hesitate, then plunge ahead. "Is that why we never visited Pakistan before?"

She sighs and closes her eyes. When she opens them again, they're brittle and shining, like two lonely stars in the still night. "When I married your dad, I had a falling out with my family. They didn't think he was the right guy for me." She laughs a strange, tiny laugh, over as soon as it begins. "They were right, of course, but I didn't really accept it until it was too late."

A sort of anger unfurls deep inside me. *Dad was perfect!* I want to shout. But of course I don't. The sleep shirt I wear has a crown with the words *KEEP CALM AND GET SOME SHUT-EYE*, but right now my blood is frothing with so many emotions. I bow my head and let my hair hang on both sides to hide my face from Mom. "I miss Dad," I whisper. "I wish he hadn't left."

If I was expecting a hug, I'm mistaken. She doesn't move. Finally, she says, "I know, sweetheart," and her voice is croaky, as if she's trying not to cry. We stay like that for a long time, deep in our own thoughts. A faint sound grows inside my head: *drum-drum-drum*.

She shakes her head as if getting rid of ugly thoughts and holds out her hand. In it is a little silver phone. "I asked your nana to get this for you. In case you get bored."

My eyes open wide. I've never been allowed a phone before. "Wow, thank you!"

"It's not really a phone," Mom adds. "But there is limited internet in case you want to play a few games or send messages to Zoe."

I shake my head. "Zoe's in Italy." *Having fun without me.*

"I know . . . but . . ." She frowns and turns to look around. "Is that music?"

Drum-drum-drum. I realize that the noise I'm hearing is coming from the street outside. We both run to the open window, but we can't see a thing. The noise gets louder, and I can make out a man calling into a loudspeaker in Urdu. "Vote for the best! Don't get fooled by the other party. You know who will give you whatever you need." The rest is drowned out by the music, shrill and startling in the night sky.

Mom grimaces, then shuts the windows. "God, these people are nuts! I don't remember the election fever being quite so high when I was a child."

I think it's sort of fun, people being so excited about electing somebody that they sing about it at midnight. Now that the windows are closed, the quietness in the room is heavy, and we stare at the darkness outside almost desperately. In the silence, I'm back to feeling the strange sadness from before. I suddenly say, "Do you know Sakina's never been to school?"

Mom frowns. "Sakina? The cook's daughter?"

I nod. I prefer to think of her as my friend rather than as a servant. I think Mom's been raised a different way.

Mom says, "Yes, I suppose so. Poor people can't usually afford to send their kids to school. They need them to work to support the family."

I feel a heat rising in my head again. "Doesn't that bother you?" I almost shout. "It's not fair!"

"I agree. It's sad. But you can't really do anything about it, can you?"

I don't answer, just close my eyes and pretend to yawn. She reaches over and pulls me into a hug. "I love how you care about other people," she whispers in my ear, and the memory of that long-ago day in Macy's comes rushing back. I push her slightly, and she loosens her grip.

"Okay, kiddo." She gets up, and I feel the mattress shift. "Don't stay up too late, my wonderful, kind daughter."

I keep my eyes closed even after she's gone back into her room. I know she's just trying to cheer me up with her over-the-top praise, but I can't help feeling it's all a big fat lie. If I was so great, then Dad wouldn't have left me. Isn't it supposed to be impossible to leave your own child if you really love them?

I stay like that in my bed for the longest time, counting sheep, then cats, then dogs, finally cows. Maybe if I help Sakina with her admission test, God will reward me by bringing back my dad.

And maybe pigs will fly.

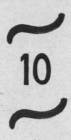

10

SAKINA
THE ENGLISH TEACHER

My first lesson is in the kitchen the next afternoon. Everyone else in the house is either asleep or resting, except for Samia Ji, who went out somewhere after lunch. Mimi watches her leave from the staircase, all sad and quiet. Then she turns to me and says too brightly: "English, anyone?"

She's right: it's the perfect time to learn some English. I'm so excited I almost forget to chop the potatoes for dinner. I tell Mimi to wait while I get things done.

"I'll help you," she says cheerfully, and I stare at her. Maybe she said something else. I often mistake the simplest of English words.

She laughs and translates in Urdu. "I. Will. Help. You."

After another moment of incredulity, I give up. Americans are very strange. We get to work, she peeling potatoes and then handing them to me for chopping. I can't help peeking at her sitting next to me, the peeler held expertly in her hand. She scrunches up her eyes as she focuses, just like Jammy as he stacks up his rocks for a game of pitthu.

Mimi looks up and catches me staring. "What? I help my mom cook on the weekends."

I try to imagine this girl in a kitchen, bending over a sink full of dishes. "What do you cook?" I ask.

She shrugs. "Lots of things. Meat loaf. Alfredo pasta. Avocado sandwiches."

I don't know what any of those things are, but they sound delicious. I half close my eyes, pretending to be an American girl with a white chef's hat and a pink apron around my waist, cooking for an adoring family.

"What's your favorite?" I ask her.

She thinks. "I like baked salmon the best." She sees my expression and explains: "It's a sort of fish."

My mouth waters, reminding me that I didn't eat more than a few bites of lunch before Begum Sahiba called me to make chai. "I like fish," I say dreamily.

"The best part is I can cook it myself. It's really easy. Just slap on some pesto sauce, arrange some peas and carrots around it, and throw it in the oven."

I'm trying to follow her even when she doesn't make any sense. Slapping sauce, throwing food into ovens? "Sounds violent," I say, not sure if she's serious.

Mimi doesn't get it at first. Then she starts laughing, huge laughs that make a happy echoing sound around us. I study her as if she's a science experiment. Her smile is like a thousand-watt lightbulb. Her eyes crinkle at the corners, and her mouth is so wide-open it looks like it's splitting in happiness. Her shoulders shake and tremble.

I'm not sure what to do. I usually watch people laugh at the dinner table, or in cars on the street, or from the windows of fancy restaurants. I don't think I've ever laughed in this huge, belly-clutching way. My laugher is usually contained within my body, hands over my mouth to keep it from spilling out.

Nobody told me happiness is infectious. Before I know it, I'm giggling too. My mouth drops open and my eyes crinkle just like hers, and my belly shakes. The sound of giggles fills the kitchen like so many bubbles, and I wonder if anyone in Begum Sahiba's house has ever laughed like this. Not since I've been working here, at least.

"Shh!" I whisper in between giggles. "Your grandmother will be very angry if she sees us like this."

Mimi tries to catch her breath. "Like what?" she

asks. "Peeling potatoes?" That makes us both sit up a bit straighter. The potatoes! I pick up the peeler I dropped on the table and get back to work, smiling broadly. She sighs like a balloon deflating happily in the air. "I knew you'd smile eventually," she tells me with a smug look on her face.

"I smile sometimes," I retort.

We peel the rest of the potatoes. At intervals I take little glances at her, and at other intervals I catch her doing the same thing. "Ready to practice your English?" she asks when all the potatoes are chopped and the table is as clean as it was before we started.

My stomach gives a rumble, as if I've eaten something left out in the sun too long. Ready? I suppose I'm as ready as I'll ever be. I nod once. Then again, more firmly.

She takes out a notebook with a pink cover. "I'll say a sentence and then you copy it."

"What is your name?"

"What is your name?"

"My name is Mimi."

"My name is Sakina."

"How are you?"

"How are you?"

"I'm very well, thank you."

"I'm very well, thank you."

"What's the weather like outside?"

"What's the weather like outside?"

"Not too bad today."

"Not too bad today."

She grins at my accent, until I turn the tables on her and ask her to speak in Urdu. Her accent is so bad it's like she's acting in a spy movie whose trailer I sometimes catch on Sahib Ji's television. I dissolve into giggles again, each bout of laughter easier than the one before it.

"What are you laughing about?" She pretends to be offended.

I shake my head, holding my sides. "You don't know much Urdu, do you?"

She sticks out her tongue at me, a habit she seems to have. "No, but I know a little bit of Spanish from school and Korean from my friend Zoe. Hola. ¿Cómo estás?"

I pause and stare at her, my laughter gone. "You learn different languages at school?"

She nods. "*Hola* is Spanish for 'hello.' Or . . . *salaam*, I guess."

I file this in my brain for future reference. "Hola. Salaam. Hello. Now I know how to say this in three languages."

She beams at me like a proud amma. "Excellent! You'll pass that test in no time!"

I'm pretty sure she has no idea what she's talking about, but her smile reaches out and touches my heartstrings in just the right way. "So tell me more about your school," I say.

"What do you want to know?" She shrugs as if it's such a boring, unimportant thing. "It's just like any other school."

Sometimes I wonder about this girl. "I haven't been to school, so I wouldn't know what that's like," I say.

I try not to sound harsh, but my bitterness must show because she immediately looks downcast. "Oh, yeah, sorry." She taps her pencil to her chin, thinking. "Well, it's a big brown building with lots of rooms to study in. And long hallways with lockers for the older kids . . ."

"What are lockers?"

Her brow wrinkles as if working on a puzzle. "Uh, they look like narrow closets with locks on the doors, and each student gets one to keep all his or her books and stuff inside. Lots of elementary schools don't have them, but mine was different."

I try to imagine rows of closets with books and *stuff* inside. I'm dying to know what *stuff* is, but she already thinks I'm stupid. Then she adds, "For example, in my locker I have a mirror to check my hair, and a few stuffed animals in case I'm having a bad day at school, and a bag of peanut M&M's for when I'm hungry. And all my notebooks, of course."

The pictures dance through my mind, and I let out a sigh. "What else?"

"Hmm, let's see. There's a music room with all sorts of instruments on the walls, and an art room with a ton of paints and crayons, and there's a gym where we play sports."

"What's your favorite sport?" I ask. "I heard that American girls love to play tennis."

She gives me a strange look. "Tennis? No, thank you! I like soccer the best, but we have to go outside into the public field across the street to play that."

On the way home, Abba wants to know what I've been up to with Mimi all afternoon. "You were so distracted, Sakina," he shouts over the noise of the traffic swirling around us. "That's not like you."

"Mimi was telling me about her school in America," I shout back, smiling a little into his back.

"School? What do you care about school?"

My smile slips away. "Nothing," I mumble.

He's silent the rest of the way. We reach home, and he parks his motorcycle on one side of our verandah while I lock the door behind us. Jammy rushes up and clings to his legs, shouting, "Abba! Abba!"

Amma is bent over the stove, sweat running down

her face. "Dinner is almost ready," she calls out. "Wash your faces, get that grime of the roads off, and sit down."

I know she means only Abba. My job is still not done. I go to help her with the chai, but Abba pulls me back. "Listen, Sakina. There's no point in learning too much about how those Americans live. It will only make you unhappy with your own lot in life."

I want to tell him it's too late: I've been unhappy for a long time. But I look away and nod. He will never understand, nor will Amma.

It's only at night, when everyone is asleep, that I let my imagination run wild. I lie awake next to Jammy's warm little body, imagining Mimi's beautiful school. I run on the field where she plays soccer, which is Pakistani football. In the art room, I draw her and me laughing together, and I sit in a classroom listening to a white, golden-haired teacher give lessons in English. And finally, I go into the hallway to my locker, where in the middle of all my English books is a glass bowl full of peanut M&M's.

11

MIMI
UNWANTED GUESTS

"Where on earth is your mother, Mimi?" Nani asks as I come down the stairs from my bedroom a couple of days later around noon. She looks even more vexed than usual, if that's possible. She's draped in a bright orange sari decorated with white sequins, and her hair is a perfect bun encased in a black lace shell. Around her bony arms, a multitude of silver bangles glint in the midmorning light.

"Um, she's gone out somewhere in a taxi," I say. "As usual."

"Again?"

I make a face. "Don't complain to me, I'm as mad about it as you are! This was supposed to be our summer vacation, but she hardly ever takes me with her when she goes to all these mysterious places."

Nani is patting at her hair, and I'm distracted by all her bling. "Why are you dressed up?" I ask.

Her hand stops. "Why are you *not* dressed up? We have guests coming soon, your mother is nowhere to be found, and you are wearing . . . that!"

I look down at myself. True, my T-shirt is a bit threadbare, and has a picture of Cookie Monster asking *WHY YOU DELETE COOKIES?* but that's no reason to get mad at me. I had no idea we were having guests. "I'll go and change into my orange shalwar kameez," I tell her brightly. "You and I can entertain the guests together, all matchy-matchy."

She looks at me as if I've lost my mind and marches away, shouting "Tahira! Is the drawing room dusted properly yet for my cousins' arrival? If I find you sitting on your behind chatting with the cook when I get there, I will fire you!"

Alarmed, I run back up the stairs to change. I rummage in my suitcase and pull out the only shalwar kameez I brought with me from Houston, an orange embroidered cotton tunic with white pants we'd found on a trip to the Indian supermarket before last Eid. The lady in the store had called out, "Buy one, get one half-price," in her thick Indian accent, and Mom had ended up buying a red-and-gold ensemble for herself too, only she has never worn hers.

It takes me all of five minutes to get dr... having all the fancy accessories Nani owns, so ... out my journal.

Dear Dad,

Let's play a game of what's your favorite. Do you know how to play it? I ask a question about your favorite something, and you have to respond with the first thing that comes to mind. Quick, what's your favorite clothes? I bet it's T-shirts with corny sayings on them. Me too. What's your favorite food? Pizza? Cheeseburgers? I have to admit chicken pulao is getting to be on top of my list. It's yummy but not spicy.

Mom's favorite food is sushi. Did you know that? Raw fish rolled in seaweed. Gross.

Maybe when we meet one day we can all go out to a restaurant together. Wouldn't that be nice? Only it can't be the Olive Garden near my school because once I ate too many breadsticks and threw up right there on their tiled floor. I can still remember how mad the waiters looked, because they had to clean up the icky mess. It was so embarrassing!

I may be on their blacklist now. So we'll just go somewhere else.

Would you like that? Going out to dinner with me, I mean.

So far, I haven't been out much in Pakistan, which is driving me nuts! I wish we'd visit different places, see different things. Anything. We're having guests today, Nani's cousins, which makes me wonder how many other relatives who I didn't know existed will I meet here? It's sort of exciting, even though it's nerve-racking!

Come to think of it, I don't know anything about your side of the family either. Your parents, your siblings. You.

Like I said, nerve-racking.

Love, Mimi

The guests are late, which Sakina tells me is quite normal and even expected. "If they say noon, they will arrive by one o'clock." She's wiping the nice china in the dining room with a cloth, then handing the plates to me to set around the table.

"I remember going to a wedding in Houston one time, and everyone else showing up really, really late," I say. "Mom called it Desi Standard Time."

She looks at me, offended. "Is that a joke?"

"It's not funny to you?" I ask. Sakina never gets my jokes.

She goes back to her wiping. "Your jokes are never funny."

I nod wisely. Time to bring her off her perpetually

high horse. "It's called 'lost in translation,'" I tell her.

"What is lost? Nothing is lost." She huffs and turns away.

I'm about to ask what her problem is. The back door opens and Mom comes in, a sheepish look on her face. Her patterned indigo tunic is wrinkled and stained with paint. "Sorry I'm late," she whispers, a finger to her lips. "Don't tell Nani."

She's got a happy-but-rushed look on her face, and I'm dying to know where she's been. But Nani's anger surrounds the house like a cloud. I wave to Mom. "Better get ready quickly. And wear something very nice—Nani is seriously dressed up!"

The guests are even later than Sakina had predicted. My stomach is rumbling, and I sneak little bites of naan from the kitchen under Sakina's father's amused eye. To distract him I say, "Salaam, how are you?" in my most polite voice.

He replies, "God is wonderful to me, Maryam Ji."

Sakina passes by just in time to hear him, and she rolls her eyes behind his back. I stuff naan in my mouth to hide my giggles.

The doorbell rings imperiously, as if the guests are mad at themselves for being late. Tahira runs to open the door, Nana and Nani close behind, and I trail after them all, searching for Mom. "Now, this is my cousin and his wife, so remember to be very respectful," Nani warns.

I can't wait to see what Nani's cousin looks like. I imagine a thin man wearing a cloth wrapped around his body, sniffing the air as if it's stinky. Does he look like Nani? Do they have similar names? I realize I have no idea what Nani's name is, or Nana's.

Mom sneaks up behind me and joins the procession. "Made it just in time!" she whispers.

I turn to inspect her. She's wearing the red-and-gold outfit she bought with mine in Houston, and she looks terrific. "Buy one, get one half-price, baby!" she whispers, and all the annoyance I've felt toward her the last few days melts away. Almost. I slide my hand into hers. I'm not going to think about her keeping secrets from me right now. I'm going to pretend everything is okay and we're having a nice vacation in the land of our ancestors.

Tahira has opened the door and is ushering two people inside with a bow. The woman is short and stout, with perfectly styled shoulder-length jet-black hair, dressed in a pale green sleeveless shalwar kameez that's tight and short. The man is half-bald, dressed in a brightly colored Hawaiian shirt stretched over a big tummy. Only when he walks past me do I realize that the shirt is pure silk, just patterned in a Hawaiian style. Nani greets the two with fake air-kisses, and Mom smiles a bit too brightly, if you ask me. "How was your Paris vacation, Hameed?" Nani asks her cousin.

He grunts. "The place was literally overrun with tourists."

We settle down in the fancy drawing room with polite little smiles at one another. Or at least the adults smile. I want to look at the bride dolls in the glass showcase again, but I'm too far away from them. I console myself with watching the adults from my corner, unnoticed for the time being.

"So, Samia, how's your painting coming along, dear?" the woman asks Mom. Funny how everybody who meets Mom asks about her painting, as if it's a strange little activity that must be addressed as soon as possible.

Mom smiles politely. "It's going well, Auntie. Thank you for asking."

"We're so jealous of your daughter's artistic abilities," her husband tells Nana, who beams with pride.

"And this is your granddaughter—how cute!" the woman gushes, reaching over to pinch my cheeks. "Which city do you live in, darling?"

"Houston," I say, pulling away from her spiky nails.

"Oh, Texas is too hot for us," the man says. "We only

ever visit New York City. Our son works in Manhattan, you know."

"Don't forget our daughter in LA, dear," the woman reminds him. "It's fun to visit Disneyland with the grandchildren, isn't it?"

"Those spoiled little American grandchildren," the man grumbles. "I hope you know Urdu, Mimi. Our grandchildren don't know a word of Urdu; it's so disgraceful."

My head is beginning to hurt with their noisy enthusiasm, but I nod. "Yes, I practice sometimes with Sakina."

The man frowns. "Who's Sakina, your sister?"

Nani clears her throat in warning. "Just a neighbor," she trills, and changes the subject.

The man in the fake Hawaiian shirt lights a cigar and puffs on it. "Samia, why don't you make the trip to New York in the winter, dear?" he says. "We'd love for you to meet our younger son."

I wrinkle my nose at the smell of the cigar. I can see Mom trying to take shallow breaths to avoid the smoke.

His wife leans forward. "He's single and doing very well as a doctor. And still very handsome."

Nani smiles a huge smile, like a shark about to eat dinner. "How lovely, isn't it, Samia?"

Mom chokes and tries to smile back, but she looks like she's about to throw up.

I can't take it anymore. I creep out of the room and into the kitchen. Sakina and Tahira are pouring curries into porcelain dishes, while Sakina's father chops cucumbers into a glass bowl. "They want to set up my mom with their youngest son," I say to no one in particular.

Tahira snorts. "They're out of their minds. Their youngest son is almost fifty years old."

Sakina giggles loudly.

I glare at them. "It's not funny." Then I think of Mom's throwing-up face as she realized what this meeting was about. "Okay, it's a little bit funny."

SAKINA
ICE CREAM FOR THE SOUL

The loud and heavily perfumed guests have finally left, and I'm washing the dishes before Abba and I get ready to prepare dinner. The evening sun is already low in the sky, and the asr azaan sounds outside. Mimi runs into the kitchen, grinning. "Mom and I are going out for ice cream. Do you want to come?"

Apparently, Mimi doesn't understand my position in her household. Servants don't get to go out for ice cream with the mistress of the house. It's just not done. "I can't. I'm busy," I mumble.

Mimi sighs and turns to Abba. "Can you please tell Sakina to come with us?" she begs, making pretty eyes at him.

Abba smiles back. "Of course, Maryam Ji. She can go."

I give him a dark look, but he ignores me. I make Mimi wait until two more pots are washed, then wipe my hands slowly with a towel on the counter. "What's the big deal with ice cream, anyway?" I mutter. "It's not that great."

Turns out that I'm totally, completely wrong. Malik, the driver, takes us to what Mimi's mother calls her old haunt, a fancy restaurant on the Clifton seawall with deep yellow lighting, long bench seats, and blue velvet curtains on the windows. A tiny bell tinkles a merry welcome above the door as we enter. And the ice cream. Rows of round buckets full of splashes of color and the most exotic of names, in a glass counter stretching the entire length of the shop. Cool Peppermint. Strawberry Sunrise. Marshmallow Fudge. Midnight Chocolate. Pistachio Delight.

"What would you like, Sakina?" Mimi's mother asks me, and my throat is suddenly dry.

"Um, strawberry?" I say, even though I have only a vague idea what this is. A fruit of some sort, red, but too expensive to do anything but admire from a distance.

"Good choice." Mimi's mother turns to Mimi. "What about you, young lady?"

Mimi is staring at the buckets of ice cream with serious eyes. "I think I'm going to have Marshmallow Fudge because it combines two of my favorite ingredients," she finally announces. The person at the counter, a young man with a nervous smile, scoops out our ice creams and we carry them to a bench. I walk as if I'm on eggshells, worried that the frothy pink delight in my hands will fall and ruin the whole experience.

Mimi has no such qualms. She's chattering, and she almost stumbles once. My heart skips a beat and I catch ahold of her arm to stop her from falling. She turns and dazzles me with a grin. "Oops, sorry!"

My first bite is a taste of sweet heaven. I munch slowly, letting the cold goodness ooze between my teeth and onto my tongue. Is this how Mimi felt when she took her first bite of mango? Finally, I swallow and open my eyes. Mimi and her mother are both staring at me expectantly. "Is it good?" Mimi asks eagerly. "Is it better than other ice creams? What would you rate it on a scale of one to ten?"

Her mother raps her gently on the wrist. "Leave the girl alone."

Mimi grins at me, then takes out her silver phone and snaps pictures of our ice cream. "Perfect," she says.

We eat in silence, which is what befits such a delicious treat. Mimi's marshmallow—whatever that is—must be good because she's licking her spoon diligently. "So those guests were interesting," she finally says, breaking the silence. "They wanted Mom to marry their old, bald son."

Mimi's mother groans. "We don't know if he's bald," she protests.

Mimi nods seriously. "Did you see his father? Baldness runs in your genes, you know."

"Well, it's not happening," Mimi's mother tells her firmly. "This matchmaking is one of the things I used to hate about Pakistan when I was a young girl. Everyone wants to come visit you, talking about their son or their cousin or their brother. It's annoying."

I can't help myself. My curiosity gets the better of me and I blurt out, "Didn't you marry your husband that way?" and I can almost feel Mimi turn into a statue next to me.

Mimi's mother has also noticed her daughter's reaction. She frowns slightly at Mimi and says, "I met Mimi's father in the States, far away from the watchful eyes of my parents and all the other matchmakers."

"You mean by yourself?" I'm amazed at how different things are in Mimi's America. I've never heard of anyone making a love marriage except in Begum Sahiba's Urdu dramas, and those heroines never fare well. "How did you find him?"

She sneaks another look at Mimi, then squares her shoulders. "Well, I met Tom at a fundraising dinner for refugees," she tells me slowly. "I was the artist commissioned to paint a few pieces for auction, and he was one of the many reporters writing a story about the program. He interviewed me for the story, and we found that we really enjoyed each other's company. Later, he called me and asked me to have dinner with him. The rest, as they say, is history."

Beside me, Mimi seems to be in a sort of frozen pain. "You never told me this," she whispers. "I've asked you so many times, and you always blow me off."

Mimi's mother finally turns and looks straight at Mimi, her eyelids heavy with regret. "I'm telling you now."

I'm lost in the images of a fancy gathering in America, with tall paintings on the walls, and handsome young men walking around arm in arm with beautiful women. Someone walks into the ice-cream shop, and the twinkling of the bell dissolves my thoughts. I cough and look down at the table. Everyone else does the same. I wish I'd never asked this question. I wish I'd just remained quiet and eaten my strawberry ice cream in peace. Mimi pushes aside her half-eaten cup and sniffs. I think she's crying, but can't be sure because she's turned away toward the windows.

I bring some ice cream home for Amma. Mimi's mother insisted on it, and I couldn't think of any reason to say no to her. The packet is bulky and cold against my thighs on the ride on Abba's motorcycle, but he's faster than usual, and the air around us is cool.

"You have to try this ice cream, Amma!" I announce as soon as I get home. "It's the most delicious thing I ever tasted!"

"More than your abba's cooking?" she teases. She's mending a torn dupatta, but she puts it down to take the spoon I'm holding out to her. "Mmmm, mazedaar!"

"I want to try!" Jammy cries, jumping about, pulling on my arm.

For a second I falter. If I don't share with the others, I'll have the entire cup to myself. Who knows when I'll ever have this scrumptious ice cream ever again? Then Jammy's hopeful face melts my heart, and I pass the spoon to him. "Be careful," I warn, making my face stern. "If you drop even a tiny bit, I won't give you any more."

When the ice cream is all finished and Jammy settles down for the night in the bedroom, I sit with my parents under the evening stars. Abba lies on the bed, legs crossed. Amma works on her sewing, back bent over the fabric. There's some noise from outside—many of our neighbors don't sleep until after midnight—and the occasional promotional cry in defense of an election candidate, but it's quiet for the most part.

"How did you two get married?" I ask suddenly, remembering the conversation in the ice cream shop.

Amma looks at me, startled. "What kind of question is that?" She scoffs. "The matchmaker brought your father's information to my parents, and I said yes. End of story."

I'm strangely disappointed. "That's it?"

Amma is getting annoyed—I can tell by her frown. "What else do you need? Flowers? Bells? Singing and dancing? That only happens in movies, Sakina!"

I shake my head. "It happens in America," I insist.

She sighs in exasperation. "Well, this is not America, is it?"

Abba opens his eyes and sits up. "Don't get angry at the poor girl. She is just asking for some details. Some spice in the food to make it interesting. Aren't you, my love?"

I sense one of his stories coming. It's been a very long time since I sat on his lap and listened, enthralled, as he told a tale handed down from his father and grandfather. I remember those stories, the one where his mother sold her best shoes to buy roti for her hungry children, or the one where his uncle walked six miles to reach a sister's wedding. Long tales with twists and turns, and ups and downs. And giant villains in the shape of rich men with mustaches. "Yes, please tell me!" I beg.

Amma shakes her head and goes back to her sewing. I cross my legs under me and lean against the wall. Abba clears his throat and begins. "I was a young man in my late twenties, owner of a small food cart in Saddar that was doing pretty well. We used to sell samosas and bun kabab and gol gappay, do you remember, Aisha?"

Amma shakes her head. "It was disgustingly unhealthy food. I don't know why anyone bought it."

"Oh, they bought it, all right. I was famous! They came from far and wide to eat my food. Men working in the nearby offices, and students from the nearby colleges, and even women doing their shopping. They all came to my cart when they needed a break. And one day my mother said to me, 'You should get married and start a family before you get too old.'"

I clasp my hands. "And you did everything your mother told you, didn't you?"

"Well, of course I did. She was a great woman, full of wisdom and excellent advice."

Amma rolls her eyes, but thankfully Abba doesn't notice. He always gets caught up in the memory of my grandmother. "You look like her, you know, Sakina."

"Yes, you've told me, Abba," I say, impatient. "Get on with the story. How did you choose Amma out of all the women out there?"

"Ha! How could I not?" He pokes a finger at Amma's

back, and she smiles reluctantly. "Your amma was my next-door neighbor, and we used to play together when we were children. I always knew I'd marry her when I grew up."

Amma finally puts down her sewing. "Enough with this story," she says firmly. "It's not even true. The truth is that I felt sorry for you tending to your lonely cart every day, and decided to marry you and put you out of your misery."

Abba laughs a deep, tender laugh. "Hai, Aisha! That is probably very true."

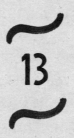

13

MIMI
MOM IS MOVING ON

Mom has decided that we must go shopping. "That orange kameez you had on the other day was much too tight," she announces on Saturday morning as I laze around on my bed in my pajamas. "Seems like you've grown quite a bit in the last year."

"I don't want more shalwar kameez!" I groan. I'm pretty sure she's saying this only because she feels guilty about what happened at the ice-cream parlor. "We hardly ever wear them in Houston."

"Well, this is not Houston, is it, my dear?" she tells me, pulling me up from my bed. "Come on. Get dressed. We've got a full day ahead of us."

I gaze longingly at my bedside table, where my journal to Dad is waiting. I'd planned on writing a summary of last night before I forgot every detail of the matchmaking meeting. Nani's cousin and his wife were hilariously annoying, like characters in a storybook. Mom gives me a little push toward the closet. "We need to get you out of those silly T-shirts you're always wearing," she says.

I'm immediately horrified. "No way will I ever give up my T-shirts!" I gasp. "In fact, I will go with you on one condition only. I want to buy a T-shirt with a funny saying too."

She pauses, thinking. "I doubt you'll get something like that here. Pakistani people don't really have a sense of humor."

I'm sure she's exaggerating. "Deal?" I insist.

She finally nods. "Fine! Now get dressed!" Then pretends to be angry when I do a little victory dance on the floor.

After breakfast, there's another problem. No driver. "Your mother just sent Malik on a mission to buy some mangoes for her all the way from Sabzi Mandi," Nana tells us, coming down the stairs with a thick book in his hand. "He won't be back anytime soon."

My ears perk up. "Sabzi Mandi? Isn't that the name of that grocery store we go to sometimes in Houston?"

Mom replies dryly: "This is the original Sabzi Mandi. An open-air market for fruits and vegetables. It's gigantic." She turns to Nana with a determined look on her face. "No problem! If Malik isn't here, we will travel old school."

I'm left wondering what old school means in this case. Walking? When she literally drags me out of the house and onto the street, I'm convinced. "It's too hot, Mom, and I'm pretty sure this counts as child abuse."

She gives me a highly amused look and keeps walking. "Not too far, silly. Just to that corner where the rickshaws are waiting."

I peer into the distance. Despite the early hour, the heat is already striking down on my head with a vengeance. I'm glad I decided to wear a cap with the colors of the rainbow on it. My T-shirt has a matching rainbow, but it's coming out of the mouth of an angry unicorn. "What's a rickshaw?" I ask.

"You'll see."

A rickshaw is a small triangular-shaped car big enough for a driver in the front and two or three passengers in the back. The sides are open, so even when we climb in, I clutch Mom's hand in case I fall out when we move. Mom bargains in rapid Urdu while I look at my surroundings and snap pictures on my silver phone. The seats are red plastic, and the partition between the driver and us has colorful metal bars decorated with streamers. The roof has a variety of happy animals painted in such a way that they seem to hang upside down above me. I see a panda and a pony, a parrot and a dolphin, all smiling as if they're happy to see me ride the rickshaw with them.

The price is finally agreed upon, and the driver starts the engine. Mom shouts, "Hold on!" and we're off in a roar that fills my ears. "Isn't this fun?" Mom smiles as if she's found some long-lost treasure of her childhood. I want to answer her, but it's too noisy, and the entire carriage vibrates as if we're in the stomach of a mechanical whale bent on destroying us. I make do with clinging to the bar in front of me, then I grit my teeth and pull back my lips to express my excitement.

"I bet they don't have anything like this in Italy, right?" Mom shouts.

"No, only gondolas and things," I reply.

"Did Zoe reply to your messages?"

I don't say anything. No need to tell her I haven't messaged my friend yet. What's the point? She's probably lost in the beauty of European fashion and culture.

In what seems like hours, we reach the mall. It's a posh-looking building, rising up to three stories high, with all sorts of designer store signs hanging from the windows. Levi's. Nike. H&M. My mouth must have been open, because Mom whispers, "Stop looking so shocked," and pulls me in. The rickshaw roars away in a movement that probably broke the sound barrier, and

I shudder to think how we're going to get back home.

But first, there's lots of shopping. I'm happy to have Mom all to myself after the activity of the last few days. Nana's house seems full of people all the time, and I miss it being just the two of us. Besides, I haven't seen Mom this carefree in a long time, smiling at shopkeepers, letting me try on different outfits, actually spending money without a worried look on her face. "Are you sure we can afford this?" I whisper when she buys my fourth shalwar kameez, a white frothy cotton outfit with multicolored lace on the hem.

She nods. "The exchange rate is ridiculously good," which doesn't explain a thing to me except that we're shopping in a way we haven't ever before in Houston.

We roam the mall like giddy teenagers, holding bags on our arms. We pass by an American clothing store, and I remember our deal. "T-shirts!" I shout, and drag her inside.

"Come on. You don't really want to buy another stupid T-shirt, do you?" she says, pouting.

"Yes, I really do." There's a rack of T-shirts in the back, but most of them have logos of big brands. I find the salesperson. "Do you have any T-shirts with funny sayings?"

She nods and smiles, then disappears in the back for a minute. When she returns, she's holding a big box

99

full of clothes. "Most people don't want funny slogans messing up their clothes," she explains.

"Exactly!" Mom says. I frown at her and rifle through the box while she checks her phone for messages. It's very disappointing. There are several Garfield shirts, and a few with Urdu cartoons on them.

"You were right," I finally tell Mom. "No sense of humor."

She smiles a satisfied little smile. "I'm always right. Now let's get some food!"

The mall food court is on the third floor. We order KFC and wait at a table. Mom keeps looking at her watch. "Are you waiting for someone?" I joke.

It's not funny, though, because just then a man strides right up to us and smiles at Mom as if he's known her forever. "Samia! Sorry I'm late." His English is smooth and accentless, not like most people who seem to be working hard at pronouncing the words.

My mouth is open this time for real. Who is this person? He's medium height, with strands of gray in his hair just like Mom. His blue jeans are gleaming clean, and his black-and-white-checkered long-sleeved shirt is crisp despite the heat outside. He drags out a chair and sits down without asking. "So how have you been?"

Mom's face is . . . radiant. "Alhamdolillah," she simpers, then turns to me. "This is my daughter, Maryam.

We call her Mimi. And darling, this is Sohail. We used to be friends in college."

"Before you abandoned me and left for America, you mean!" Sohail laughs.

I close my mouth and scowl ferociously at him. Who is he to joke and laugh at my mom, and call her by her first name as if he's someone special? Mom is supposed to be sad and worried, pining away for Dad, not laughing with a strange man who she apparently arranged to meet here. The scowl is useless. They're turned to each other, chattering in an effortless mixture of Urdu and English about their college days. What fun they used to have. How interesting life was before kids and marriage and graying hair.

Ugh. I want to throw up.

"So what class are you in, Mimi?" Sohail asks, turning his million-dollar smile in my direction. "Or, grade, as they say in America."

I debate ignoring him. Or better yet, saying something very sarcastic. Mom gives me a stern look. "Going into sixth," I mumble.

"Oh, middle school," he replies as if it's the best thing in the world. "What are your favorite subjects?"

I can't believe he's trying to get to know me, or at least pretending in order to please Mom. "I don't know," I say, and rummage through my shopping bags as if I urgently need to find something. He nods like he perfectly understands the predicament of choosing a favorite subject in middle school, and turns back to Mom. They're sitting so close it's nauseating.

Our food arrives, but I hardly touch it. I can't wait to go back to Nana's house, even if it means riding in that noisy rickshaw one more time. But of course, the universe is not on my side. After we're finished eating, Sohail offers to take us back home in his car, and Mom says yes immediately.

Double ugh. I make another attempt to ditch this guy. "But I loved riding on that rickshaw!" I grumble.

Mom turns and frowns at me. "Really? You looked like you were going to puke."

Sohail reaches for our bags and hefts them all up with ease. "My car is much less noisy, I promise," he says. "This way, my ladies."

Triple ugh.

14

SAKINA
TELL ME A SECRET

The kitchen is bustling with activity, the fragrance of sizzling tikka boti permeating the air. Abba has a technique of grilling that involves placing a hot coal into a pot of meat when it's almost cooked, and I'm eager to see how he does it. *The taste of the grill without the hassle*, he's told me many times.

The boneless chicken is cut into neat squares, and marinated overnight with tikka spices, yogurt, olive oil, and ginger-garlic paste. It's been simmering on a bed of onions and tomatoes for an hour now, and I'm guessing it must be soft enough to melt in my mouth, if I was allowed to eat the same food as the owners of the house. Now, Abba heats some coals on the stove and gently adds them to the pot, taking care not to disturb the beauty of the chicken inside.

We—Tahira and I—lean forward to look. "Stand back and give me space," Abba tells us.

"Smells delicious," I murmur, saliva pooling in my mouth.

"Aaaargh!" I hear a scream and freeze.

Tahira jumps. "Who is that?" she whispers, afraid.

I scoff. "Sounds like Mimi. I'll go check."

Upstairs in her bedroom, Mimi stands on top of the bed, a look of horror on her face. "Sakina, be careful, there's a snake in here!"

I look around. Her clothes are lying on the floor in an untidy heap. The top of the wardrobe is scattered with all sorts of things: scrunchies, lotions, small stuffed animals attached to keychains, and a cap with a rainbow on it. "That's impossible. How would a snake get in here?"

She's practically crying. "I saw it, I'm telling you. It was this long." She holds up her hands about three inches apart in front of her face. "It wiggled and slid all the way under those clothes."

I sigh. "Maybe don't leave your clothes on the floor like this?" Then I bite my lip hard because a servant can't say that to the granddaughter of the mistress of the house.

Her shoulders slump. "I know, Mom always tells me the same thing."

I move her clothes with my foot. I don't believe there's really a snake in her room, but it's always better to be safe. Something wiggles underneath and I jump back. "See, I told you!" Mimi shrieks from the bed.

"Shh! You'll scare it," I hiss. I look around for something heavy and find a pair of clunky black shoes with red bows. I hold a shoe tightly in one hand. Then I go back to the clothes, picking them up one by one and dusting them off very carefully. No sudden movements. No sounds. When the last piece of clothing is left—a pair of striped capri pants I've see Mimi wear many times—I smack the shoe on top of it.

Mimi screams again, but not as loudly as before.

I stop smacking and pick up the pants carefully, shaking them a little. "You can stop screaming now," I say. "It's a centipede."

She comes down from the bed and leans in to look. "Wow, you're so brave!" she whispers in a scared little voice.

I bend down and pick up the centipede with my bare hands. "It's not dead. Don't worry," I tell her. "Your pants softened the blow. It's just stunned." I take the slimy thing out onto her balcony and fling it down, watching it land on the grass. It shakes its little body and slithers away.

"Thank you," Mimi says awkwardly.

I point to her capri pants. "You should put those in the laundry basket."

She cringes and nods. "Sure," she says, but I see her eyeing the trash can in the corner of her room, so I'm guessing that's where they will end up. She flops down on her bed, sighing. "That was a close call."

I'm not sure what she means. "It was a centipede," I say.

"I'm not in my right mind since Saturday," she tells me, or rather tells the ceiling she's staring at angrily. "Everything here is strange, the fajr azaan wakes me up way too early every morning, and now my mom apparently has a new boyfriend. Life sucks."

I'm sure she's being dramatic. I'm learning that dramatic is Mimi's preferred style. "If you close the windows tightly before going to sleep at night, the azaan won't sound as loud to your ears," I tell her. "And what boyfriend are you talking about? Your mother is such a nice person; she'd never do anything scandalous like that."

She makes a frustrated little sound in her throat. "She met this guy at the mall the other day. Sohail somebody. He used to be her friend when they were in college." She sits up and looks at me with teary eyes. "You should have seen them, laughing and talking as if I wasn't even there. It was disgusting. I'm sure they're going to meet again and again, the whole time Mom and I are in Karachi."

I can't understand what she's saying. Isn't Mimi's mother married? Boyfriends are something from movies and dramas, and I can't imagine Samia Ji doing anything so inappropriate. Plus, she's old like Amma, not a teenage girl. "You're just being sensitive, I'm sure," I soothe her. "Americans are very friendly, aren't they? Not reserved and silent like Pakistani people. Your mother is just being a normal American."

Mimi chews her lip, thinking. Finally, her frown disappears and a smile crosses her lips. "I think you're right. She's way too old to have a boyfriend anyway!"

I know she wants to talk some more, but I have work to do. I turn to leave. "Lunch is almost ready; you should come downstairs."

Tahira and Abba have a good laugh when I tell them about the centipede in Mimi's bedroom. "Imagine being scared of a little thing like that," Tahira says, grinning widely. "That girl is hilarious."

Abba shakes his head. "Don't make fun of Maryam Ji. She's very new to this country. It's difficult to be away from your home, you know."

I'm still remembering his words when I take chai and zeera biscuits to the family room in the late afternoon.

It's a sunny room overlooking the back garden, with tall windows on three sides, and a big lazy fan that swishes around and around in slow motion. Sahib Ji spends most of his day here, especially since he retired a few years ago. He's got a big television—the one I sometimes watch when I get a chance—and a bookshelf full of books that are very dry and boring, with pistons and engines on the covers. I've tried reading those books. They are good for nothing besides falling asleep quickly.

Sahib Ji also has another passion: chess. He's tried to teach me how to play, but Abba always calls me back to the kitchen just when I'm starting to get the hang of it. It's a game of strategy and patience, both of which servants have little time for. We spend our days putting out fires, answering others' beck and call, and generally running around worrying how things will get done. Who has time for a long, drawn-out chess match, where the goal is to protect the queen and sacrifice the pawns? It seems too close to real life to be any fun.

Mimi seems to be enjoying it, though. She's sitting on a chair with her legs crossed under her, leaning forward until her nose almost touches the chess board. Her eyebrows are furrowed into deep slashes, and her lips purse together. She hardly looks up as I set the tray of snacks on the sideboard in the corner. "Thank you, dear," Mimi's mother says. She's sketching in a notepad near one of the windows, her lips pursed in an exact replica of her daughter's.

Dear? I pause, not sure how to answer. It's nothing, really, but her simple words spread into my chest like warm milk in the middle of the night. "Yes," I whisper, not sure what I'm agreeing to.

I pour chai in two cups and hand one first to her, then to Sahib Ji. He takes a noisy sip and clears his throat. "So, where is Tom these days?" he asks Mimi's mother.

From the corner of my eye, I see Mimi's hand tremble midair. She seems stiffer, the angles of her face harder. Who's this Tom person Sahib Ji is talking about?

Mimi's mother shrugs, but the movement is also stiff, like cardboard. "I don't know. He's a South Asian political expert, apparently, so he could be anywhere, really. Seems like he was in Karachi recently."

"You're right—he moved to Karachi last year," replies Sahib Ji. "I've been enjoying his political analysis in the newspaper. But I haven't read anything from him for a couple of months now. Not even about the election."

I can't stop staring at Mimi. If a person's entire being could be focused on one conversation, this would be it. Rapid breaths. Flared nostrils. Frozen hands. But she keeps staring at the chess set in front of her as if that's all she can think about.

Who is Tom? What's he doing in Karachi? And why does Mimi look as if her insides are shattering like brittle glass on a windy day?

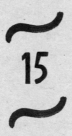

MIMI
I'M FINE, EVERYTHING IS FINE

I can't breathe. My left eye twitches until the chess pieces in front of me are dancing as if bewitched. Why are they talking about Dad?

I focus on the knight Nana's just moved, not wanting to disturb the peace of Mom's sketching. Wanting to disappear. I bow my head until it's almost touching the pieces. I like the way everything else leaves my consciousness, and the only thing in my vision is the chess board.

Mom shrugs again, an action I can literally feel. It's a shrug that's second nature to her, one she performs whenever someone says something she doesn't like. "Maybe he's moved on to somewhere else by now. It's what he does best."

"Samia . . ." Nana begins. Then he stops and hides his face in his teacup.

Mom goes back to her sketchbook. "Why do you even care, Abba? You didn't want me to marry him in the first place. Let's not talk about this now; it's ancient history."

My hand trembles in my lap. Dad in Karachi? How is that even possible? Wouldn't I have felt his presence when I drove the streets from the airport? Wouldn't my heart have leaped at sharing the same space as him?

Nana harrumphs like a horse with a mouthful of tea, and I strain for more of anything. More details. More answers to the buzzing questions in my brain. But there is silence, neither father nor daughter in the mood for much conversation. The delicate tinkling sound of teacup against saucer echoes loudly around me, jarring my nerves.

"Checkmate!" Nana announces in triumph. I lean back, loosening my grip on the arms of the chair I've been sitting on. "You don't usually play this badly," he adds, but he says it kindly, as a joke.

I grin—maybe—and stand up. "I have to pee," I tell him, uncaring that this is not a word one uses in polite Pakistani company. Mom had told me so on the plane to Karachi. *Don't use words like* poop *and* pee *and* fart, *please, in front of your grandparents.* It had sounded hilarious at the time, but now I suddenly wonder if she was just trying to calm her own nerves with such advice.

In the bathroom off the hallway, I stare at my pale face in the mirror. My pink T-shirt says *I'M FINE. EVERYTHING IS FINE. NOW LEAVE.* which is so off-point it's aggravating. Zoe gave it to me at the end of fifth grade as a hooray-we-finished-elementary-school gift. I got her nothing, mainly because I didn't know giving presents on the last day of school was a thing.

"I'm pathetic," I tell myself severely in the mirror. "Dad's been in Karachi all this time and I didn't even know."

"Your T-shirts often lie—do you know that?" Sakina's reflection joins mine in the mirror, and we stand silently together in the tiny bathroom side by side. She's darker than I am, a true Pakistani. I'm half-and-half, making the chai weaker and less authentic.

"I'm fine," I insist, but my red eyes mock me.

"Who was your grandfather talking about?" she asks.

I want to tell her to mind her own business. But her face is actually concerned, her cheeks puffed in a way I've seen before, when Nani is shouting at her or her abba is feeling ill. I sigh and sink down on the edge of the bathtub. "My dad . . . my father."

"He's not back home?" She looks confused, as if the

thought of a father not left behind weeping as a daughter goes to another continent for vacation is unheard of. "Where is he?"

I realize that Sakina knows almost nothing about me. Most people don't. It's usually difficult for me to tell others about Dad, but her face is just the right amount of worried without being even a tiny bit nosy. I want to tell her the truth. "He left us when I was five years old. I know he moves around a lot because of his job, but I've tried to keep track of him all these years."

I stop, thinking of my late-night Google searches every few months, the world map I keep in the back of my closet with red dots on the countries he's reported from over the years. Tanzania. Iraq. Mali. Libya. Wherever there is conflict and war, my dad is there, like a brave warrior.

"And?" Sakina prompts.

I blink, and my voice slows. "And . . . Nana just dropped the bombshell that Dad's right here in Karachi!"

She digests this carefully. I can see her forming the words with her mouth, making sense of them. "What is he doing here?"

This is suddenly a good question. "He's a journalist. He writes news stories for the paper." I stand up so suddenly I almost shove Sakina into the wall. "I need to find out what paper! Can you get me old newspapers or something? Can you help me?"

She straightens up, looking suddenly uncomfortable. "I . . . don't . . ."

I grab her arm. "Come on! I'm helping you with your English, aren't I? You can help me too!"

"I can get in trouble right now for not preparing tonight's dinner in the kitchen," she whispers loudly. "Why don't you just use the internet?"

I make a pleading face. "It's not been working since last week. Nana said the cable was cut by thieves and they're waiting to get it fixed."

Sakina grumbles under her breath about hooligans on the streets, then asks, "What do you want me to do?"

"Well, what's the biggest English newspaper? Surely you must know that!"

She bites her lip as if I've asked her a very difficult question. "There are so many. *Dawn*, the *News*, the *Express Tribune* . . ." Her voice trails off as if she's said too much.

I rush past her, out of the bathroom, and upstairs to my room. The door is open. Mom is standing inside with her arms crossed over her chest as if she's prepared for battle. Too late.

✻ ✻ ✻

"I guess you heard," she says, closing the door behind me.

I pace the room, ready to fight. "About what? About the fact that everyone knows more about Dad than I do? Like the fact that he's been in Pakistan the whole time and I didn't even know. Like . . ."

I want to scream, but my voice wobbles and my throat is tight. *I will not cry*, I tell myself. I stop talking and take deep breaths. Crying is not a good look for me.

Mom unfolds her arms and walks toward me. "Oh, kiddo, I'm so sorry. I didn't want you to know."

The tightness in my throat disperses. "Is that supposed to make me feel better?" I shout. "How can you keep this a secret from me? You have no right to—"

Oops. She's mad now too. "I do have a right, Mimi! I'm your mother. That man left us with no thought of you or me, or anyone else except himself. He got a call about an assignment in Afghanistan—or Iraq, or someplace with a war—and he packed up and left. He loves a good news story more than he loves me . . . us!"

I almost waver in my resolve, but I stand strong against her indignation. "You should have told me he was here," I insist, softer this time.

She seems suddenly deflated. She sinks down on my bed. "Yes, I should have," she admits. "I was going to, as soon as we settled in and got rid of the jet lag and everything."

Worst excuse ever! I got over my jet lag days ago, and she's been traipsing around town with this Sohail person. I cross my arms across my chest to let her know I'm not fooled.

She continues with an earnest look, reaching out a hand to me. "Also, in my defense, I didn't know where he'd gone until much later. He's been traveling constantly, as far as I know, going from one dangerous region to another. I didn't know he was in Karachi until very recently, when your nani told me on Skype about an article she'd read in *Dawn*. Believe it or not, I was too busy trying to keep our lives afloat to track that deadbeat's movements."

Dawn! That was one of the newspapers Sakina mentioned. Could it be Dad's paper? I sit down next to Mom, taking care to keep my distance. "Why did we come here, Mom, really?" I ask gently. "Because of Dad?"

She recoils from me as if I've said the words *poop*, *fart*, and *pee* all together in the same sentence. "No! Never!" she exclaims in anger.

"Then why?"

She stands up, a hard look on her face. "I thought you should get to know your grandparents. I thought it was time for me to stop fighting with my own family.

Honestly, I was so busy with my job search I didn't even remember that your . . . father . . . was here. But apparently you think everything in the world is about you!"

I watch her stomp out of Uncle Faizan's room with angry steps.

Dear Dad,

This is going to be very short. I am hopping mad, as my neighbor Mrs. Peabody says. I recently found out Mom's biggest secret. I'm still processing it, but I'll be sure to tell you soon enough. When I found out, she got super mad, although I should be the only one who's mad right now. Isn't that typical Mom?

One more thing. I finally see the resemblance between Mom and Nani. They can both get pretty furious, pretty fast.

Mimi

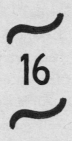

SAKINA
THE EVIL WITCH

Begum Sahiba is furious, and it's all my fault. I knead the dough for parathas with quick, desperate hands as she looms over me, frothing at the mouth. "Faster, you lazy oaf! You were supposed to have kneaded this dough an hour ago! It's after twelve now. What have you been doing all this time?"

I'd been practicing English by myself in the shed outside, sounding out sentences Mimi had written down for me at our first lesson. The words were lumpy and uncertain in my mouth, like a food I've never tasted before. *Would you like some sugar in your tea? It looks like it will rain tomorrow, so you should take an umbrella.* But the thrill of taming them made me forget all about the time. Made me forget I was a servant bound by my duties, and learning a new language is not supposed to be on my priority list at all.

Begum Sahiba's shrieking pushed me out of the shed and into the kitchen, horrified. I'd forgotten to knead the dough for the potato-filled parathas Abba was making for lunch. Abba should have reminded me, sure, but he isn't feeling his best these days. I've noticed he looks more tired after small tasks. At the moment, he's sitting on a stool in the corner of the kitchen, eyes closed, head resting against the wall, breathing shallow puffs.

I sneak little peeks at him as I knead the dough. The lady-dragon raps my head with her hand. "Stop looking here and there! Work faster. This dough needed to chill. You know that, silly fool!"

I agree with her secretly. If the parathas aren't as good as they should be because Abba used warm dough, I'll be in for an even bigger scolding. I think quickly. "I could make some chaat while the dough cools," I say. "Just a noon snack so that nobody will mind if lunch is a little late."

She glares at me. She's wearing a blood-red sari with a pattern of black flowers all over. "Hmph, chaat!" she huffs, but I can see she's listening.

"Some nice chaat with the special masala you like," I add, wiping my forehead with my sleeve. "And also maybe some homemade potato chips and ketchup for Mimi."

Begum Sahiba glares at me again but walks away toward the kitchen door. "Hurry up and finish the dough, then get to work on the chaat," she barks. "I'll let everyone know there's going to be special snacks in fifteen minutes."

There's no way I can have the snacks ready in fifteen minutes, but I nod and pummel the dough with both hands. Abba groans from the corner and Begum Sahiba stops. "Is he all right? What's wrong with him?"

"Nothing. He's just tired," I answer quickly, hoping it's the truth.

She looks at Abba for a long minute. "We have guests here, Ejaz. You can't afford to get sick, you hear me?" she tells him, but her voice is soft, almost concerned. Am I hearing her correctly?

He nods and smiles. "I'm perfectly fine, Begum Sahiba. The parathas will be ready at two o'clock sharp."

He does seem better. Maybe all he needed was a bit of rest. Begum Sahiba leaves with a parting reminder: "Tell Tahira to help you with the cooking today. Let your abba rest."

I try not to let my mouth hang open with shock. "Yes, ma'am," I mutter, knowing I'll never ask Tahira. Her annoying stories and repeated questions will only add to my frustration. Abba has trained me well; I can handle a day of cooking without his help if need be. I pat the dough into a metal container, wrap it with plastic, and put it in the fridge to cool. Then I get to work on the chaat, mixing boiled chickpeas, potatoes, and spices together with lemon juice and vinegar for a tasty snack. After a while, Abba gets up and joins me at the stove, frying potato chips by my side.

"You don't have to, Abba," I protest. I don't want him collapsing on me.

He waves me away. "Don't be silly. I'm fine now. Let me help you."

I still remember the first time Abba and I cooked together. I was almost seven, and he took me to his job. Amma wasn't pleased, because I usually helped her in the house.

"You can do without her for a day," Abba told her, grinning. He was always grinning, always happy. Still is. With all the hardships he's witnessed in his life, I find that incredible.

I snuggled behind him on his motorcycle all the way to the house. It was a single-story villa, with a mother, a father, and a houseful of children. "I'll get to work on the family's lunch," Abba told me when we got there. "You chop some vegetables for the salad."

I wonder now at my seven-year-old self, using knives and china plates. Amma never let me use a knife at home. *If your hand slips, there will be lots of blood*, she always warned, making me wonder if it was out of concern for me or her own distaste at the sight of blood. But Abba thought I was a big girl. He clapped after I finished chopping all the lettuce, cucumbers, and tomatoes. He hugged me when I washed the knife carefully and put it away. Then he called me to the stove.

"Come. This will be your very first cooking lesson," he told me in a low voice, full of joy and expectation. He dragged a stool right next to him and pointed to it.

I joined him at the stove—it was a small one, not half as fancy as the steel giant in Begum Sahiba's kitchen—and watched as he stirred a pot full of chicken curry. He handed me the spoon. "You stir while I pour in the yogurt," he said.

I watched as he dropped clumps of white yogurt into the chicken. Then I carefully stirred and mixed the chicken together until it was blended well. I stood by his side and we watched the curry bubble merrily, thin streams of tangy flavor tickling my nostrils and making me breathe deep. I don't remember how long we stood together, staring at our creation. After a while, I got tired and rested my head against his shoulder, and he put his arm around me.

"How would you like to cook with me every day?" he

asked, and I nodded so vigorously we bumped heads. "*Uff!* I suppose that means yes!"

Now, standing together in Begum Sahiba's kitchen, I wonder if Abba remembers that scene from so long ago. "You got lucky this time with Begum Sahiba," he tells me, and his voice is gruff. "She's not always so understanding."

I roll my eyes, but only because he's looking elsewhere. "So what else is new?"

He shakes his head. "She's not so bad, you know. You just have to get to know her. She's got a kind heart underneath all that anger."

"If you say so."

He looks at me, suddenly serious. "What were you doing outside all morning anyway?"

I want to tell him so badly my heart thumps. He's always encouraged me to do my best, to be better than this life I've been born into. But leaving the job to study in a school will be unacceptable to him, I know. "Nothing," I mutter. "Mimi gave me some things to look at."

"You and Maryam Ji get along well, eh?"

I focus on the chaat. It needs a sprinkling of black pepper, perhaps some more salt. "She's okay. A bit spoiled and clueless, but that's to be expected."

He chortles. "I'm happy you've found a friend your age. She looks like a good girl."

I remember the conversation in the bathroom the day before, Mimi's crumpled, anxious face. "She's lonely, I think," I tell him. "Imagine not having an abba to hug every night."

He smiles at me, his face creasing into the lines I know so well. "Why don't you take her out to visit a few places? I'm sure Sahib Ji will allow you to go with Malik in the mornings. He's very trustworthy. He's been with the family since he was a teenager."

My hands stop midair. "What about cooking?"

He waves me away. "I think Begum Sahiba will be very happy to spare you for a few weeks, if it means entertaining her granddaughter."

I doubt that Begum Sahiba can scrounge up even an ounce of generosity or kindness, but I take his word for it. He's looking very confident. "I'll talk to her," he adds.

The chips are done, and he takes the sizzling wok off the stove. "Hand me that newspaper from the pantry, will you? There's a stack of old ones lying on the upper shelf."

Newspapers? I rummage in the pantry, thinking about Mimi's father, about Mimi's request to find her old newspapers. Abba's holding out an impatient hand,

and I hurry to him. The oil from the chips needs to be absorbed in paper, an old kitchen trick from his food cart days.

Abba loads the snacks on a tray as I go back to the pantry. The stack of newspapers is half a mile high at the back. Mimi's anxious face and red eyes loom in my mind. This is turning out to be an excellent day, despite all of Begum Sahiba's shouting.

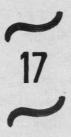

17

MIMI
A STRANGER IN MY OWN LAND

"We're going sightseeing!" Sakina announces the next day as she clears away the breakfast plates.

I'm busy inhaling my fifth (or is it sixth?) French toast cooked desi-style in fresh ghee, so I think I haven't heard her correctly. "Going where?"

She stops, uncertain. "Isn't that what you say? Sight-seeing? When you want to see the sights?"

I nod, remembering my pledge to be her teacher. In the avalanche of emotions of the previous few days, I've forgotten about her English lessons. "Oh yeah, that's absolutely correct. Good job!" Then I pause. "What sights? I didn't know there were any sights to see in Karachi."

She frowns, her mouth a silent slash against her

cheekbones. "Of course," she says, as if I'm stupid. "There are many, many sights. So many!" She raises her arms wide to encompass the entire dining room. The dishes clang in protest.

I look around the room. The rest of the family has already retired to their rooms, doing whatever they do after a coma-inducing breakfast. "Okay," I say, slowly. "But I have a ton of questions. How will we go? Who will take us? And will you go as well? What about your job? Is this your idea, or will Nani be shouting again?"

A panicked look spreads across her face. "Stop! You're speaking too fast!" she tells me frantically. "One at a time, please?"

I take deep breaths. The thought of escaping this mansion and sightseeing in fresh air has made me a bit dizzy. "Did. You. Ask. Anyone's. Permission. About. This?" I enunciate. "And by anyone, I mean Nani, obviously."

She relaxes and resumes her task of stacking plates one on top of the other, building a dirty little Tower of Pisa. "Yes. Abba asked Begum Sahiba, very nicely, and she thought it was a good idea."

I look at her doubtfully. That the cook would have clout with the dragon lady of the house, when all others feared her, is kind of amazing. Also slightly unbelievable. Maybe this is a classic case of miscommunication due to a lack of English skills. "Are you sure?"

She nods and balances the plates on her arm, her face serene. "Yup," she answers. Then she adds helpfully: "That means yes."

I grab half the plates from her and stride toward the kitchen. "I know."

I get dressed speedily, before anyone changes their minds about this sightseeing outing. I brush my hair until it swings around my face like a static curtain, then put on my best jeans and a maroon T-shirt with the words *JUST BECAUSE I'M AWAKE DOESN'T MEAN I'M READY TO DO ANYTHING*. I pocket the little phone Mom's given me and a roll of rupees. At the last minute, I sling a black-and-white leopard-print scarf around my shoulders. It's a different look than my usual, but if I'm going to be walking among the masses, I need to look the part.

Mom's bedroom door is ajar as I walk past. I peek in. She's sitting at the desk, writing on some papers. I haven't really talked to her much since our last argument, so I hesitate at the doorway. "Um, I'm going out with Sakina and Malik for a little while," I say.

She hardly looks up. "Yes, your grandfather told me about the plan. It's a great idea. Have fun."

She doesn't look like she means it. "What are you doing?" I ask.

"Nothing much. The new job in Houston gave me some paperwork to complete, that's all. I had to print it out from the copy shop since the internet's still not working." She puts down her pen and sighs. "Listen, I wanted to say I was sorry about erupting at you the other day. I shouldn't have screamed. None of this is your fault."

I'm not sure if I'm ready for this conversation. My feelings about her secret and about being in the same city as Dad are still boiling inside me. I hope she doesn't know I didn't sleep a wink the night before.

Well, maybe I slept a few winks. Not many.

"It's okay. I understand," I mumble, even though I really don't.

"Are you sure?"

I smile brightly through gritted teeth. "Sure." I say, and leave. I'm pretty sure she's staring at my back, but I'm not going to turn around and check. Just seeing her face has sucked some of my happiness out, leaving me like a deflated balloon someone left at a party. Every time I see her now, I think of her secret. Of Dad.

Dear Dad,

I think it's finally time to let you in on the secret. I know where you live! All this time, I'd thought you were lost, like a puppy or a bracelet or something. In kindergarten when Zoe asked me how come I didn't have a dad, I told her that you were an explorer who traveled the world, and that you somehow got amnesia and didn't remember how to come back home. Isn't that silly? Every year when my elementary school had Donuts with Dad, I'd make excuses to stay home, so that not even Mom realized what the deal was. One time I faked a racking cough that alarmed her so much she actually took me to the doctor! Poor Mom, or so I thought. Now I've discovered that she knew where you were, probably knew how to contact you, and that even my grandparents were in on the secret. Everyone except stupid old Mimi.

The question is, what do I do with this new info? Do I go looking for you, or do you want to stay hidden? I feel like I already know the answer.

Mimi

Nana's car stands gleaming in the driveway. The white-haired and long-bearded driver, Malik, holds the door open for me. "Ready, Maryam Ji?"

"Are we going out alone?" I ask him, slightly alarmed. Mom never lets me go anywhere alone, not even to school.

Sakina pulls me inside. "You have me and Malik here—no need to worry!" she says. Malik bows and closes the door behind me, his face solemn but friendly. We start reversing down the driveway, past the house and out of the gate that Tahira's holding open for us, waving excitedly. I wave back.

"That's right, Maryam Ji," Malik says. "I will take good care of you two."

The car has an air conditioner, but Sakina insists on rolling the windows down. "You can't get the whole experience if you're behind glass," she announces.

I glare at her. Sweat is already forming little droplets around my hairline. "I will literally die from the heat," I tell her.

"Nobody can die from just this little bit of heat," she answers very seriously, as if I'm the one learning a new language. "You can sit in your air-conditioned room when you get home to America."

I sigh, thinking of our cramped Houston apartment. The noisy street outside, the leaky toilet. Last summer the AC was on the fritz all July, and it was as hot as Karachi. "America feels so far away right now," I murmur.

"What?" she leans toward me to hear better.

"I said, where are we going today?" I shout in her ear, and she recoils. I laugh, a weight lifting from my shoulders. Maybe this outing will be good for me, help me relax and forget about Dad-related things.

We leave Nani's house behind, zooming through the streets. I see the sign that says Sunset Boulevard, and it reminds me once again of Dad. Tendrils of anger and a sort of panic rise within me, but I squelch the feelings. Not right now.

The traffic becomes thicker. There are motorcycles like the one Sakina rides to work in the mornings. Buses and cars, all blowing their horns emphatically, all too close to us. The air whips at my scarf, making it flap. "Is this safe?" I worry aloud. "There's a lot of traffic. Why is there so much traffic?"

She grins. "Welcome to Karachi," she says, and even Malik turns and smiles at me.

I turn back to look out the open window. There are so many buildings, each taller than the last. I read out the signs. *OCEAN CITY MALL. BURGER TIME. PIZZA PALACE.* A parade of vans with flags and music blaring from the rooftops whizzes by. "Election rallies," Sakina explains with a dismissive hand. "They think music and noise will make us vote for them."

I stare at the vans disappearing in the distance in clouds of smoke, remembering the midnight music fest from the week before. "Who are they?"

"Who cares? All the political parties have similar rallies. They beg and plead for our votes, but none of them actually want to get anything done."

I look at her. She's got this hard look on her face that makes her seem older than both of our ages combined. Her life is so different from mine, I suddenly think. She actually works for a living, contributes to her family, has an opinion about grown-up things. I, on the other hand, just exist. If I dropped dead tomorrow, nobody would miss me.

Well, Mom would miss me, but that's not what I mean.

"What will happen if you're admitted to that school you were talking about?" I ask her. "You won't be able to work anymore, right?"

She seems startled, as if the thought has never occurred to her. Or maybe she's just shocked I've figured it out, innocent American girl that I am. She looks down at her hands in her lap, twisting her dupatta into knots. "I suppose you're right. No more work for me."

"What have your parents said? Will they be okay without your income?" It's such a weird thing to be asking a girl my age. None of my other friends work, unless you count Zoe getting a dollar for each chore she does in the house. Mom has never paid me for chores, despite my begging.

She looks out the window like a convict dreaming of escaping a prison. I think for a second she might jump out of the car, but she stays put. "I haven't told them yet," she whispers.

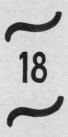

18

SAKINA
WHITE WALLS AND GREEN GARDENS

Mimi asks a thousand questions a minute. I think it's because she's American, and American children are unnecessarily carefree and independent. I've watched a movie here and there, heard about something called the Kardashians on the radio. American children don't follow the rules, never stay silent, and always talk back. Disrespect is an accomplishment to them, and chaos is fun.

Mimi isn't that bad, of course. She's kind and funny, and her T-shirts are always interesting, even if sometimes they make little sense to me. And she's always asking questions in a breathy voice that can be annoying if you get too much of it. Still, she's grown on me like a mushroom grows in the grass after a good rain.

She wants to know all about my admission test, which I really don't want to discuss. I'm almost completely sure Malik cannot understand English, but he's constantly peeking at us in the rearview mirror, and I don't want my secret to get out. So I whisper and tell her that I've been planning to surprise Amma and Abba once I pass the test. If I pass it.

She frowns. "Keeping secrets from your family isn't the best idea," she whispers back, and I'm reminded that she's got family secrets of her own she's upset about. Her mother's secret. I blink, trying to look unconcerned. I've never known a girl whose father left her before, unless you count my second cousin in Rawalpindi, whose father—my uncle from Amma's side—died in the war in Afghanistan.

We reach the mausoleum of Quaid-e-Azam, the founder of Pakistan. I admit, it's a cheesy place to take a visitor, but it's my very favorite place to be even in the heat. Malik parks the car under a tree and says, "Stay where I can see you, okay?" then promptly leans back in his seat and closes his eyes. We giggle at him, then leave the car before he changes his mind.

The weather is cooperating today—brisk wind, cloudy sky—and we scramble out into the deep grounds that surround the mausoleum. We climb up the steps together and walk around until we reach the huge triangular structure with its gentle arched doorways. I resist the urge to hold out my arms and say *ta-da* like they do on television shows.

Mimi is staring at the mausoleum with wide eyes. Her dupatta flaps in the breeze like it's waving madly at the burial place of our country's most beloved man. "Impressive!" she breathes, her eyes sparkling.

"I told you!"

We walk to the building, and then back again, skipping down the steps. I stumble and almost fall, and Mimi has a fit of giggling. She brings out her silver phone and takes dozens of pictures, some with me in them, some without. She tries taking selfies, but she's laughing too much, and the phone keeps shaking. What is it about this American girl that makes me so prone to laughter? We finally collapse on the grass for a rest, our faces shiny with sweat and something close to happiness. Mimi's short hair is in disarray, and there are sweat stains on her maroon T-shirt. She looks less like an American girl and more like . . . me. I stare at her, then turn away when she catches me looking.

Malik huffs up with a bag, then leaves again to go back to the coolness of the car with a wave. Abba's packed us some food—leftover French toast and red apples, a bag of roasted peanuts, and a thermos full of chai—and we munch on everything like old friends who've been visiting people's graves together for years.

"I wish I could stay here forever." Mimi sighs.

"What do you mean? I'd have thought you'd be dying to go back to your country," I tease.

She considers this. "Well, I miss home, definitely," she says. "I miss school and my friend Zoe, and everything that's familiar and ordinary. But . . ." She sighs again and scrapes at the grass with her shoe. "Lately things have become so complicated."

"You mean Sohail?"

"Ugh. Don't even remind me of that man!" She sits up, animated. "What is his problem? Why did he even have to come into our lives? Why did Mom ever contact him?"

Like I said, Mimi asks so many questions. "Did you ever consider that your mother might be lonely?" I venture.

She scowls at me. "How can she be lonely? She has me."

I don't know what to say. She knows the answer; she's just being stubborn. I let it go, and we watch the grass wave gently in the breeze. A line of ants marches on the pavement nearby. "More reason for you to be happy to go back soon," I finally offer as consolation.

She's still not satisfied. "Don't tell anyone, but this place is growing on me. In the States, all I see is kids who are different from me. Mostly white kids, but also from many other countries. Here, everyone is the same. Brown, desi, Pakistani, whatever you want to call it. It feels familiar. Normal."

I'm not sure I follow, but I don't tell her that. Whenever I don't understand her, or say the wrong thing, she frowns and looks disappointed, like a kitten that didn't get the milk it had been promised. "You are only half-brown, though," I finally say, and from the way her face darkens I realize I've said the wrong thing again.

We eat in silence for a while, then Mimi brightens up and says, "Let's practice some English," so she asks me questions about the scene around me, and I think of replies. Who was the Quaid? What was his contribution to Pakistan? When did they build this mausoleum? Halfway through I realize she's just being curious, so I throw an apple core at her and lie back to stare at the sky.

Mimi takes out her phone and snaps more pictures. There's a small group of children playing tag in front of us, their cries of joy filling the air. From their clothes, they look like servants, and I'm happy their sahib jis have let them out for a while to play. Another crowd of children runs over. They're dressed in dark-gray-and-white uniforms, and their white tennis shoes gleam in the sunlight. A field trip, no doubt. The servant children become immediately shy and withdrawn, then slowly wander away, leaving the schoolchildren to play.

"They didn't have to leave," Mimi protests.

"It's not their place," I tell her, bitter. "The ones who go to school are in . . . how do you say it? . . . a better class than the ones who work on the streets or in houses. That's the way our society is."

"Well, it's backward, that's what it is!" She sits up, indignant. "This would never happen in the States!"

I don't like the way things are in Pakistan, but I also don't like how Mimi keeps comparing it to America and finding us lacking. "Yes, and here you'd never find a father leaving his daughter and going away," I shoot back. "So I suppose we're—how do you say?—even!"

Her face changes. Her eyes get hard and her chin wobbles. She stands up and brushes crumbs off her jeans, and then walks away. "Wait," I call out, and then stop to pick up all our food. She may be American, but she has gotten used to having a servant in an awfully short time.

When I get to the car, she's already sitting inside, windows closed, air-conditioning blasting. "I'm sorry. I don't know why I said that." Will she tell Begum Sahiba? I'm worried Abba will get fired for this disrespect. I'm worried Mimi will stop teaching me English.

I'm also worried I may have hurt her just as we were starting to become friends.

She sniffs and turns away from me. "Whatever."

I'm not sure what she means by this. Whatever what? Is it another idiom? A slang? "Please, Mimi?" I beg, searching my mind for something to tempt her to smile. I remember the pantry in the kitchen. "I'll help you with those newspapers you asked for!"

She looks at me from the corner of her eye. "You will?"

"Yes! I know where to get a ton of them. I promise!"

She sighs a huge sigh and smiles ruefully. "I shouldn't have called Pakistan backward. It's not."

I shrug. Right then I'd have called my own parents backward to get her to smile more. "It is backward in a lot of ways. And forward in many others. We are not so different, even if we seem to be."

"Maybe you're right."

Malik coughs loudly and starts the car. "Home?" he asks in Urdu.

"Yes," Mimi and I reply together.

"I thought he was asking me," she whispers with a start. I'm relieved to see her eyes are no longer angry.

"He probably was," I whisper back. "Since he knows you are the boss."

She lets out a small grin that brightens the car. "The

boss? I like that. In the land of the free, everybody is *my* boss."

"The land of what?" I have no idea what she's just said.

"Never mind." She leans back in her seat and closes her eyes. "You definitely need to practice your English more."

I cross my arms to stop my sudden shiver. In that moment, she looks like a smaller version of Begum Sahiba.

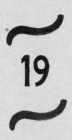

19

MIMI
A CAMEL FOR YOUR THOUGHTS

Dear Dad,

I've decided that if I want to be a journalist like you, I need to work on my research skills. I've started reading some of Nana's coffee-table books in the mornings while Sakina works in the kitchen. When she has a break, she reads with me, practicing her English. And guess what? We found a very interesting book about Karachi, the city of Mom's birth, and your current home.

I admit I'd never given it much thought before now. Mom always told people she was born in Pakistan, as if the country was one big place without cities and towns and villages. Maybe it's something people do when they don't live somewhere anymore, make it insignificant and impersonal to show they don't care.

Sakina calls where I live America, even though that's so much more than just the United States. She never remembers that I live in Houston, which is in Texas, which is in the southwest part of the US. It's funny when you think about it. Aren't we all from planet Earth? Then why are places so important?

Nana's book told me all about Karachi. It used to be a small fishing village in the 1700s, and has been ruled by so many groups since then: the Greeks, then the Talpurs, and finally, the British. Then the Quaid-e-Azam made it the capital of Pakistan when the nation was born in 1947. All around the city, you see evidence of this history: ancient European-style buildings stand next to modern high-rises, and cute little horse carriages clip-clop next to the latest brands of Toyotas and Hyundais on the roads. It's like a kaleidoscope I once made in school, all bright and colorful and slightly dizzying.

Nana said that no visit to Karachi is complete without a walk on the beach. The Indian Ocean is like a sparkling blue-green jewel, reminding me that none of my troubles—not even the fact that I'm away from you—is bigger than the sea. I think I'm going to ask Sakina to take me there. I've only been to the beach once, when Uncle Faizan visited us and Mom took us

to Galveston Beach. It was fun!
Do you like the ocean? I hope you do.
Love, Mimi

Clifton Beach is full of people, just like every other place I've visited in this city. I spy the water even before we park, and I roll down my window to smell the warm, flapping wind. "Lovely," I murmur, and Sakina rolls her eyes at me.

She didn't want to come, saying the beach was smelly and crowded. "There's nothing to do there," she complains in the car, but I shush her with a pointed finger. She has to be joking. There is so much to do and see, I'm not sure how I'll do everything.

"Mom told me about monkey dances and snake charmers and other cool stuff," I tell her. "I want to see all of that."

"What's cool about all that?" She scoffs.

"I've never seen any of those things before, that's what!" I practically shout.

I turn away from her and stare at the people outside my window. Men, women, and children crowd the sand and walk into the water, fully clothed. There's not a bikini or pair of shorts in sight. In fact, some of the women are dressed very formally, with jewelry and long trailing dupattas.

Sakina tells me helpfully, "The beach is a big deal for some people."

"Not you, obviously," I say.

She shrugs. "It's okay. My brother, Jammy, loves riding the oont."

Malik hears the word *oont* and turns around. "Would you like a camel ride, Maryam Ji?" he asks eagerly. I look at where he's pointing. Rows upon rows of camels, dressed up in wild decorative beads and blankets, wait for passengers near the seawall. My eyes almost pop out of my head, and I nod so quickly hair flies around. "Yes, please!"

He takes us to the camels and haggles with the owners while I admire the animals. Their eyes are half-closed, as if they're enjoying the breeze, and their eyelashes are longer than any human's could be. Many of them wear fancy knitted hats and neck scarves with little golden bells. I reach over and pat a camel on the nose, and it stares at me. "Hello, you beauty," I whisper.

"Stop talking to camels," Sakina hisses at me. "They can't understand you!"

"How do you know?" I counter.

Before she can answer, Malik waves to us. He and a camel owner have agreed on the price. We climb on the camel and it lurches up. Sakina and I clutch each other and screech. "Be careful," Malik warns the owner.

"They better not fall off or you'll have to answer to my sahib ji."

The owner is suitably impressed. He holds the camel's reins tightly and walks us around as if we're eggs in the shape of girls. I'm so high I can see the tops of everyone's heads. The wind flaps my scarf around, whipping it in my face, making me giggle. We walk all the way to the edge of the water and then back again, the camel swaying side to side as it strolls with us on its back.

Later, Sakina and I sit on the sand and dip our toes in the water. It's a cloudy day, and the sun plays hide-and-seek in the sky above us. "What do you want to be when you grow up?" I ask her dreamily.

She turns to stare at me. "I never thought of that before. Just . . . anything. Something. Not a cook, that's for sure."

"Your father won't mind? I think parents like it when their kids follow them in their careers."

She turns back to squinting at the water. "What about you, then? Will you be a news writer like your father? What's it called? Oh yes, journalist."

I have to think about this. Sometimes I say that to Mom, just to make her mad. But in my heart, I'm not so sure I'd like to be like Dad. Writing boring assignments from different countries? No thank you. "Maybe a local journalist, like those who stay in the same city and read the news on television," I finally reply.

She makes a serious face and pretends to read from a paper. "Breaking news from America. A young girl who's visiting the Clifton Beach was kicked by a camel because she wouldn't stop patting its head. The camel's owner demanded hundreds of rupees to compensate for his animal's stressed-out feelings!"

I let out a peal of laughter. "That camel was totally enjoying my patting!"

"It looked like it was about to run away and hide under the rocks."

Malik gestures from the car, and we stand up reluctantly. We're almost to the car when Sakina says, "I think I'd like to be a teacher when I grow up. I already teach Jammy his sums and the alphabet. I could help so many poor children get educated."

"That's perfect," I reply, and give her a little hug for the first time.

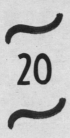

SAKINA
BUN KABAB AND CONVERSATION

I'd never tell Mimi, but the camel ride we took was the highlight of my life. I've only been to Clifton Beach a few times, and Jammy is the one who always gets the camel rides, never me. Whenever I complain, Amma tells me that before Jammy was born, I used to ride on the gentle animals, but that was so long ago I don't have any memory of it. I want to believe her, but somehow I don't.

Sakina Ejaz isn't the sort of person who walks on beaches and rides on camels. Sakina Ejaz has no time for fun.

Today is fun, though. After the beach, Mimi declares she is starving, even though I tell her she has no real understanding of what that word means. She tells Malik loudly she needs to eat something right now; otherwise she will faint. Malik steps on the accelerator and drives to a nearby street filled with open-air restaurants. The air is thick with barbecue smoke that makes my stomach grumble. "Can we sit outside on the chairs?" Mimi begs, but Malik refuses to let her.

"Someone will come to the car to take your orders," he says.

It takes only a few seconds for the car to be surrounded by boys younger than us. "Madam, you want kabab? We have the best kabab in all of Karachi!" calls one. "Chinese! Eat the best Chinese in the subcontinent!" boasts another.

Mimi's lips crumple as she tries to decide, so I help her. "Three bun kabab, please," I order, my voice sure and loud. "And one Coke."

The boys spring to action, and a thrill runs down my spine. This is what a begum sahiba must feel like, ordering foods and commanding respect with nothing more than a flicked eyebrow. I catch a glimpse of my face in the rearview mirror, and I'm shocked. My eyes are hard, and my mouth is a straight line.

I sit back and try to relax my face. I would rather be Sakina Ejaz than any begum sahiba.

"Why did you order kabab?" Mimi whines. "What if they make it very spicy?"

I realize she doesn't know what a bun kabab is. "It's not what you think," I assure her. "Wait and see."

While we wait for our food, a trail of beggars arrives in twos and threes. They are mostly as young as Jammy, with a couple of women carrying babies. Their skin is darkened by the sun and their clothes are patched and wrinkled. They surround our car, hands outstretched, lips mumbling prayers. For some reason, they look straight past me and focus on Mimi. How on earth do they know who the real begum sahiba is? She seems to shrink in her skin as she watches them. "Why are there so many poor people in this country?" she almost cries.

I'm immediately stung by her statement. "Are there no poor people in America?" I shoot.

"No. Not really." She pauses, and I can see her trying to think. "Wait, yes there are. There's a man who lives under the bridge near my school. I see him every morning wrapped up in blankets when Mom and I walk past. Mom sometimes makes an extra sandwich and gives it to him. And lots of kids in my school get free lunch because they can't afford to buy it. They have to stand in a special line in the cafeteria and only get certain foods. I bet they feel sad."

I relax. "See, there are poor people everywhere."

"But *why*?" Mimi is back to being upset. "Here, I see these beggars everywhere. Like on street corners and on the roads, and in people's houses . . ." She hiccups and stops talking.

I don't know the answer to this question. "Abba says it is the will of God," I reply weakly.

"How is that possible?" she frets, her hands worrying the hem of her T-shirt. "How can God allow some people to have everything and others to have nothing? How can He be the Creator of both Pakistan and America? The two are like day and night. God is supposed to love us equally. Isn't He?"

I sigh and nod slowly. I, too, have asked the same thing so many times. Malik is watching us from the rearview mirror. "What do you think, Malik?" I suddenly blurt. He's older than Abba; maybe he has more wisdom.

Mimi leans forward too. "Yes, Malik, what do you think?" she echoes.

Malik strokes his long white beard for a minute. Then finally, he replies: "God gives each of us free will to do whatever we want. Sometimes human beings are bad to each other. They steal and hurt and lie. They don't take care of the less fortunate."

"I don't get it," Mimi says obstinately. "These poor people aren't poor because they did something bad. Sakina didn't do anything bad!"

I'm startled to be lumped in with the beggars outside. They are so pathetic that even Amma's eyes fill with tears when she sees them, and she scrambles to find coins for them in her almost-empty purse. I've always thought of myself as better than the beggars. At least my family is making some money. At least we have a roof over our heads, even if it leaks in the rainy season. Does Mimi really see us all as the same? All poor people?

Malik gives me a little smile in the mirror. He speaks slowly so that I can understand. "Not Sakina, Maryam Ji. Our leaders. There is corruption in our leaders. That's why this election has everyone so riled up. We know that the people who are asking for our votes are mostly corrupt, lying thieves. They want to be elected to steal money and get rich, not to serve their communities. When that happens, poor people like us are the ones who suffer the most. The rich people aren't affected."

"Everyone can't be corrupt," Mimi protests quietly.

"Not everyone," Malik agrees. "But even the good leaders have their hands tied by a corrupt system."

I have a lump in my throat. "You don't know how lucky you are, Mimi, to live in America," I say. "To be rich."

She gives a snort, her tears gone. "Rich? We have no money in Houston. It's only here that we seem rich. And there's corruption in America too. Last year our mayor's assistant was caught stealing money from the city. It was in the news for days!" She's speaking in a mixture of Urdu and English, but I understand her perfectly.

Malik nods and closes his eyes, satisfied. "See, there are bad people everywhere," he tells us. "And good people too."

There's a tap on the window, and the beggars all disperse. Our food has arrived. Mimi hands one foil-wrapped package to Malik, and then opens her wrap carefully. I know she's expecting kabab, but instead she has a round sandwich with a ground-beef-and-lentil patty, mint chutney, onions, and a juicy tomato. "A Karachi specialty," I tell her, and unwrap my sandwich eagerly.

She takes a bite and closes her eyes. "Mmmmm."

"There's Coke for you too," I say, proud I've remembered what she likes to drink.

She's still got her eyes closed. "Who needs Coke when there's bun kabab heaven?"

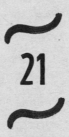

21

MIMI
TOM SCOTTS, SPECIAL CORRESPONDENT

Dear Dad,

I've been meaning to write in my journal for the last week, but I've been busy. I guess you know what that's like, so you won't mind. Sakina and I have been going out in the mornings after breakfast, doing touristy things.

Sakina can be fun when she's not acting like a martyr. She took me to see a huge old white marble mausoleum where the founder of Pakistan is buried, and since then we've visited some of the most awesome places in Karachi. We went to Clifton Beach one day, where I rode on a camel, and ate the most delicious sandwich in the whole world! We visited a huge park with rows of ancient trees, and a British-era building with a two-story library inside. We sat on a gigantic Ferris wheel that wobbled and made me scream, but the view from the top was amazing. Everywhere we went, human beings crowded around me in a way I'm not really used to, but they all smiled and waved and nodded, like they were giving me a great big hug and saying, welcome to Pakistan, Mimi, we missed you.

I should have been happy, but for some reason I kept looking over my shoulder, feeling sad. Did you ever visit these places? If I looked hard enough at the mess of footprints in the sand, would I see yours? Did you also ride the same camel or drive up the same roads as me?

Did you ever think of me, or Mom? Did you even know Nana and Nani were living in the same city as you? Did you ever want to pick up the phone and call me?

I'm telling myself yes to all those questions.

I'll probably never know the real answers.

Your daughter, Mimi

"What are you doing?"

I quickly hide the journal behind my back, trying to seem casual. Sakina stands in my doorway, holding a big box in her arms.

I remember to breathe. "It's just my journal," I tell her. "I write things in it when I'm alone."

She staggers inside and sets the box down on the floor. "What sort of things?"

I shrug, twisting my pencil between my fingers. She knows about Dad; what harm will it do to share the journal with her just a tiny bit? I pat the space beside me on my bed, and she sits down gingerly, as if it's made of live snakes. "I don't think I'm allowed to . . ." Her voice trails off.

"This is my room, and I'm giving you permission." I sound very bossy, even to myself. I stifle a giggle. I push the journal into her hands, then act cool. Nobody's seen this thing before, so if she makes fun of me, I'm not sure how I'll react.

She flips a few pages, her face still. "These are letters to . . . your father?" she asks.

I nod.

"I don't understand. I thought you hadn't met him since you were five."

I realize how silly the journal sounds. I can feel myself getting red. "I know," I try to explain. "It's just my way of writing down my feelings. He's never going to see this, obviously."

"Americans are, how you say . . . weird," she says, then closes her mouth quickly.

I have to laugh at this. "You may be right. I can see how this seems weird."

She hands me back the journal. "I still feel bad for what I said the other day about your father, though. Amma would be horrified at such bad manners."

I shrug and place the journal inside my bedside table. "That's okay. I don't really want to talk about it."

She points to the box on the floor. "That's my . . . gift . . . to you. To make you feel better."

I stare at the box. Where did she get money for a gift that big? I get up from my bed and approach the box carefully. "What is it?"

"Newspapers!" she tells me happily. "Old English newspapers, just like you asked."

I open the box and rifle through the newspapers. There are so many, and most seem to be dated this year and the last. "This is amazing! Thank you so much!" I smile so big my lips crack. "Where did you get these?"

"Turns out Abba keeps these in the pantry to absorb oil. Like when he fries chips or needs to wrap up leftover fish or something."

I sink onto the floor and take out a handful of news-papers. "I love your abba," I tell her.

She joins me on the floor. "Me too," she says, pleased. "Now, what exactly are we looking for?"

We find three columns written by Tom Scotts, special correspondent to *Dawn*. Each comes with a grainy black-and-white picture of a man with windswept hair and an open-necked polo shirt staring seriously at something in the distance. I try not to gobble the picture with my eyes. I've never seen one of his articles with his picture attached before. They've always just included his name, which I know is called a byline.

Tahira knocks on the door an hour later, announcing that Sakina's father is looking for her. "All over the house he searched," she tells us severely. "Poor man, he was so upset. You didn't hear him shouting at all?"

Sakina scowls at her and leaves hurriedly, even though I doubt her father was shouting. He seems like such a calm person whenever I encounter him in the kitchen. Once I even caught him humming a tune under his breath as he sautéed onions.

I stare at the newspaper picture of Dad after Sakina's gone back downstairs to the kitchen to cook dinner. My memories of him are so vague, so dependent on smell and touch, that I never really thought much about how he actually looks. About the way his eyebrows arch over his eyes, and his hair falls onto his forehead in a clump.

The few pictures we have of him at home are so different from this serious one. In my bedroom, there's a framed picture of Dad in his graduation cap and gown, smiling broadly. Mom says it's from when he graduated journalism school and just before he got his first assignment. It was way before I was born, apparently. There's another picture of him holding me in his arms. I'm a tiny baby, wrapped in a blue-and-white-striped towel-thing they give out in the hospital to newborns. Mom says it looks as if he gave birth to me all by himself. I'd like to think it was a proud moment for him.

I don't know how long I stay on the floor, looking at this new, journalist dad. The one who's left his family. The one who writes long, boring articles about the state of local politics after the last elections. Mom knocks on my door, *knock-knock*-pause-*knock*, and I look up.

"What is all this, Mimi?" She seems tired. I wonder what time it is. Judging from the grumbling in my stomach, it's past eight o'clock.

It's too late to hide the newspapers, so I cast around for an excuse. "Just using some old newspapers for a project," I utter, surprised at how easily the lie comes to me. She knows I'm still mad at her for hiding the truth from me. I've hardly spoken to her in the last week. While Sakina and I have been busy experiencing the sights of Karachi, Mom has been . . . out with friends.

She's frowning now. "What project?"

"Uh . . . a collage?"

I can tell she's not convinced. I've never shown even

160

an ounce of interest in art. I look into her eyes with a mix of anger and innocence, daring her to challenge me. Hoping she doesn't.

"Samia, are you coming?" Nana's voice from downstairs rouses us out of our staring match.

Mom sighs and walks out. "Time for dinner, young lady," she calls out. "Be sure to show me this mysterious collage when you're finished."

Dinner is a silent affair. Sakina and her father have already left, along with all the other servants, so we have nobody to wait on us. I'm relieved. Having silent human beings around the house picking up your things and opening doors for you is very strange.

"The servants have started leaving early because of all the election drama," Nani complains, obviously missing the silent human beings more than I do. "It's very annoying but can't be helped. The traffic gets really bad because of all the parades."

We're eating leftover goat-potato curry and chickpea pulao, or at least everyone else is. I find the goat too spicy and the chickpeas too hard. I make do with plain rice and mint yogurt sprinkled on top like a dressing, and almost all the salad. "We can eat dinner by ourselves once in a while, Ammi," Mom says, and she and Nana exchange a laughing glance.

"I keep hearing about this election everywhere I go," I say, gulping down some water. "Who are you guys going to vote for?"

Nani gives me a stern look. "Oh no, voting is for poor people. We don't vote."

Mom sets down her glass with a small thud. "Are you serious, Ammi? Why the . . . why not?"

Nana soothes Mom's hand with his. "Your mother is just being melodramatic," he says. "We will certainly vote as soon as we figure out who to vote for."

Nani adds, sniffing, "There's no point. They're all cheats and frauds, you know."

I know that can't be right. "I think the Pakistan Socialist Party is pretty good," I offer, remembering the article of Dad's I've just read. "They are doing some great things in rural areas, and they could be very good for Karachi."

All the adults turn to look at me as if I've grown two heads. I look down at my T-shirt, thinking it has something bad written on it. It's a picture of bicycle handlebars with the words LIFE BEHIND BARS written underneath. Nothing too radical, although you never know if Pakistani grandparents will appreciate the joke. "What?" I ask.

"How do you know about Pakistani politics?" Nana asks, his face a mixture of confusion and pride.

Before I can stop myself, I foolishly admit, "From Dad's columns."

Mom gasps louder than someone in a horror movie. Nani's spoon clatters onto the floor. Nana just stares at me, his mouth slightly open.

I smile weakly.

SAKINA
THE NEWSPAPER OFFICE

I have another special outing planned for Mimi today, so special that I can't stop smiling as we head to the car. Malik is wiping the bonnet down with a cloth. We climb in and wait for him to finish. "How much do you like roller coasters, Mimi?" I ask, wanting to give her a hint.

Mimi shakes her head. "No rides today. No touristy place."

She looks serious. "What's happened—everything okay?" I ask her.

She sighs louder than a cow with too much milk. "I spilled the beans about Dad's columns," she admits, twisting her hands around her scarf. Today it's a bold red polka-dotted one, over a plain black T-shirt. She's hunched over in the car, so I can't see what the T-shirt says. Something strange and not even remotely funny, I'm sure.

Spilling beans doesn't sound like a great catastrophe.

"It means tell everyone a secret," Mimi adds, seeing my confusion.

"Was it supposed to be a secret?" I ask, confused.

She looks at me as if I'm slow. "Yeah, it was. Mom gets this angry look on her face whenever Dad is mentioned. And Nani has nothing nice to say about him, ever. The other day I overheard Nana and Nani talking about the olden days, when the neighbors all made fun of them because their daughter ran off with a white man."

I pout a little to show her I'm sorry for her. "That's why you should never listen to other people's conversations," I say. "You never hear anything nice."

"Gee, thanks for the advice."

She doesn't look very thankful, but still I say, "You're welcome."

Malik puts away his cloth, gets in, and starts the car. He turns around to look at Mimi. "Where are we going today, Maryam Ji?" he asks her in Urdu.

I open my mouth to tell him, but she frowns at me. "Here," she says, handing him a folded piece of paper. "I need you to take me here today."

We're on the main road when I can't take the suspense

anymore. "Where are we going?" I ask. "I thought I was in charge of deciding."

"You're the one who told me that I'm the boss." Her mouth is set in that obstinate little line I'm getting to know so well.

"I did," I admit quietly. It's a fact I've tried to ignore. But the ugly reality of my station in life versus hers rears its head too often, mocking me. Her clothes are always so clean, and her hair always smells of a mixture of strawberry and lime. But it's the nails that give her away: short, white, and gleaming with health.

"Then wait and see," she tells me.

I curl my fingers into my palms, hiding the dirt under the nails that never seems to come out, no matter how hard I try, and wait for us to arrive wherever she's decreed. "So what was the family's reaction?" I ask, tired of the silence. How will I ever fully grasp this blasted English language if I don't talk more than two sentences at a time?

She sighs. "They were shocked. Nani kept opening and closing her mouth like a fish."

An alarm runs through me. "Did you tell her I gave you those newspapers?" I practically shout. I have no need to be in the middle of this family drama.

She shakes her head. "No, she didn't even ask about that. Just told me to stop being so interested in him."

She scoffs. "Can you imagine? My own dad! Why wouldn't I be interested in him?"

I feel my muscles relax. "I can just imagine. She's Begum Sahiba, after all."

It's a long drive, past the malls we've visited, past the museum, until we're in the financial part of town. I've only been here once before, when Abba needed to submit some documents to the bank to prove his identity. We traveled together on his motorcycle, coughing in the fumes of cars and buses, swerving to avoid busy drivers going too fast. *Everybody is busy here, Sakina,* Abba told me. *Busy working hard, making money.*

We finally stop in front of a tall white building with windows so big they take up almost the entire wall. "I'll let you out here, Maryam Ji, and park on the next street," Malik says.

Mimi wipes her hands on her lap, not moving. "Aren't you going to get out?" I ask.

She swallows once, then twice. "Okay," she says, but she keeps sitting.

Impatient, I get out of the car and walk over to her side. "I didn't come all this way to sit in the car," I tell her gently. "I could be making delicious lunch for your nani and nana right now, you know. They love eating my food!"

She lets out a deep breath and opens the door. "Nani

167

especially," she says and walks toward the building.

She still hasn't told me where we're headed. I open my mouth to ask again, but just then we get to the main doors, and I see the brass lettering on the wall. *Dawn Newspapers*.

"My friends, I'm so happy to see you all here today!"

A man with a big mustache, wearing a stiffly starched white cotton shalwar kameez, stands outside the *Dawn* offices on a little platform. A crowd of about fifty or sixty people shuffle their feet and wipe their sweat in front of him. Two things are apparent from the scene: this is another one of those infuriating election rallies, and Mimi is listening closely, her mission forgotten.

Because of course I've figured out what we're doing here by now. I may not be able to speak perfect English, but I'm not stupid. Mimi's been determined to see her father again since the minute she found out he was in Karachi. Which may be a good thing for her, but it's bound to get me in trouble.

"Mimi, let's go. We shouldn't be here," I tell her fiercely.

"Shh!"

"I'm supposed to be taking you sightseeing," I insist in a low voice. "Begum Sahiba and your mother are going to be very angry with me if they find out we're at the *Dawn* offices."

"Then don't tell them."

I grit my teeth. It's too loud here. Better to wait until this speech ends and the crowd disperses. Maybe Mimi will listen then.

Thankfully, the mustached man is at the tail end of his speech. "I promise to end poverty by providing jobs to all those who are unemployed! I promise to get rid of the scourge of nepotism, and the way rich, important people get their relatives into positions of power. I promise to clean up the streets of Karachi and fill them with beautiful trees!"

The audience claps wildly. I gaze past the crowds to the back of the building, where a big pile of garbage invites emaciated dogs and children alike. They're rummaging for scraps, and I know they are more my kin than this mustached man. Mr. Aziz. I know who he is; Abba has almost made up his mind to vote for him, despite my protests. I've seen him on television, pleading for my family's votes in his greasy voice, his party workers going around the neighborhood like an unruly army making empty threats. *Vote for Mr. Aziz if you know what's good for you.*

Abba knows what's good for him. But I'm not that gullible. I can't be swayed by empty promises of sweeping changes, when my neighborhood streets are full of garbage and flies. I'll wait and see what this election cycle brings, but I'm not hopeful. Pessimist, Abba calls me, but he knows I'm right.

Finally, after much clapping and whistling and shouting, the crowd disappears. Mr. Aziz leaves in a long black sedan the size of a poor man's hut. The entrance to the white building is suddenly wide open, the brass of the *Dawn* twinkling in the sunlight as if inviting us in. "They'll have air-conditioning inside," Mimi pants, and pulls me in.

I look at her. Her T-shirt is soaked with sweat, and I can finally see what it says. *BE A FROOT LOOP IN A WORLD FULL OF CHEERIOS.* I can only understand 50 percent of these words, but I don't ask what the rest mean. She's fiddling with her scarf as we go through the security line and get x-rayed for the sake of safety. The machine beeps, and she belatedly takes out her phone from the pocket of her capri pants. "Sorry," she whispers, her face almost white.

I forget that I was trying to convince her to go back home. I can see how nervous she is, and I remember the tears in her eyes when she was talking about her father. How can I worry about getting in trouble when she's got such a big burden? I have to help her.

I look around, then walk purposefully ahead. There's a receptionist nearby, dressed in a blue-green tie-dye shalwar kameez with a matching dupatta covering her head. Her fingernails are covered with a bright pink shade of nail polish, and the exact same shade of lipstick adorns her pursed mouth. A name tag on her chest proclaims *Rubina Ahmad* in trim black letters. "How may I help you?" Rubina asks us in Urdu.

Mimi is quiet. I roll my eyes at her. "We're looking for Tom Scotts, a reporter from America," I tell the receptionist in shaking Urdu.

She stares at me as if I'm in the wrong place, which perhaps I am. "This is not America, little girl," she tells me, sneering.

I take a deep breath. "Yes, I know that. He writes for *Dawn*." I pull Mimi's arm a bit. "She's from America. She knows him."

Rubina's demeanor changes instantly. She smiles sweetly at Mimi. "Is that true, dear?" she drawls in English. "You're from the States?"

Mimi nods, still frozen. Really, this is getting annoying. Why did she come here when she was so scared of actually finding what she was looking for? Not what, who. Or is it whom?

Rubina asks, "Do you know the Kardashians? They're so great, aren't they?"

"Um, I don't really watch that show," Mimi mumbles. I elbow her and she straightens up. "The reporter, please?"

Rubina runs her sharp nails over her keyboard. "Spell the name for me, darling?"

Mimi clears her throat. "T-O-M space S-C-O-T-T-S," she says in a tone so low I can hardly hear her. Then she repeats more loudly: "T-O-M space S-C-O-T-T-S."

Rubina frowns at her screen as if it's got rude jokes written on it. Finally, she looks up again. "Sorry, there's nobody here by that name," she tells us. But I see her eyes, and they are saying something different.

"Please, I'm sure you know him?" I plead. Mimi is back to looking very ill.

The woman turns her frown to me. "Of course not. We don't know the important reporters upstairs." She looks me up and down with curled hot pink lips. "And neither do you, servant girl."

I gulp. How do people always know I'm a servant? Do I smell? Do I give off a certain vibe? I glare back at her, unfazed. I've been called worse, and I'm with the boss girl at the moment, so I'm certainly not scared.

Rubina Ahmad goes back to her work. "Say hi to Kim K for me," she calls out.

Mimi keeps standing and wringing her hands. It's like her feet are stuck to the floor and she can't move. A security guard wanders toward us. "You girls need to leave now," he calls. "We're not allowed to give out contact information about our reporters. Safety purposes."

I take one look at his set face, and the gun he's fingering at his hip, and drag Mimi outside. "Wait," she protests, but I march out to the next street where Malik is waiting with the car.

"No. We have no business being there, Mimi," I say. "You heard that woman. Your father doesn't work there."

"But that's not true. You saw the newspapers. He does work there! Or at least he used to." She's almost crying, refusing to get into the car. Somebody honks from behind us. Malik honks back and shouts, "Patience, man! Can't you see the little girl is upset?"

I open the door of the car and push her inside. "We have to go, Mimi."

We drive away, and I turn my face to the other side so I don't have to see the tears gushing out of her eyes.

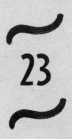

23

MIMI
RED EYES AND A RESOLVE

As the days pass, my head seems to be exploding with knotty little thoughts scurrying around inside my brain. The only good news is that Nana's internet has finally been fixed, so I spend the weekend deep in my bedroom, doing all sorts of online searches that take forever to load. Tom Scotts. An actor in New Zealand. A guy in a police uniform in England. The president of some farm association in Iowa. A YouTube star called Tom Scott without the *s*. I never realized how common Dad's name is.

I try Thomas Scotts, *Dawn* columnists, Karachi, Pakistan. At least that gets the right results, but there's nothing worth mentioning. A few articles he's written, a few images I've seen before. Absolutely zero about a wife and daughter in Houston, Texas.

"Ugh!" I shout more than once. "Tell me something I don't know, universe! Tell me where to find him."

The universe, of course, is silent. Unless you count the blaring election parades that pass by the house every night like clockwork. "I wish I could just get on one of those cars and drive away," I grumble. Nana's birds sit in the tree outside my window, beaks open, tweeting what they think of me.

By early next week, the parades have started driving by the house in the afternoon as well. The people with loudspeakers are even louder, more musical and emphatic, reminding us all to vote for their candidates. "Less than three weeks to go," mutters Nani darkly one day, "before all this farce in the name of democracy will be over and done with."

She's joined us in the family room as Nana and I attempt another game of chess. She usually takes a nap in the afternoons, but Mom has been going out almost every day now, and Nani has been taking her place quietly in the corner near the windows, examining the oil paints with a disdainful hand. "Have you decided who to vote for?" I ask, aiming for a cheerful tone.

Nana gives me a warning glance. "No use talking politics to this one, my dear."

Nani waves her arm at us, her bangles glinting in the

sunlight. "It's all right. I've been doing some research as well," she says. "Your bombshell the other day about reading your father's writings made me realize that we all need to get a little bit more educated about the issues that face our country."

I abandon the chess game and go sit next to her. "Can you tell me about my dad, please?" I beg, making a pretty face. "Mom hardly ever talks about him."

She sniffs. "What do you expect? He was quite useless as a husband and provider, you know."

Nana coughs loudly, but she shushes him. "Oh, he was. No use denying it!" She turns to me. "I'm sorry if it hurts your feelings, dear, but we tried telling your mother not to go through with it."

I harden my heart. I need to hear these things. "Go on, please," I whisper.

"What else is there to say? The neighbors gossiped all year long, saying we couldn't find a good enough match for our daughter and so she had to settle for some white man far away. Said we were bad parents for letting it happen. I couldn't step foot in the Karachi Gymkhana for months without people turning and staring at me."

Nana lets out a shout of laughter. "Oh, come on, dear, it wasn't that bad. People gossip all the time."

She shakes her head with regret. "They just wouldn't stop. I was so glad when Major Tahir's granddaughter

176

eloped with that butcher boy. Gave them someone else to talk about."

I walk back slowly to the chess game, wondering. Did Mom feel sad about the neighbors' gossip or her parents' shame? Is that why she never came back to Pakistan after she got married?

Nana nudges me. "Your turn, daydreamer!"

I sigh. "It's no use. I suck at chess."

He pulls my hair gently. "Nobody—what do you say?—sucks at anything until they decide that it is so."

I roll my eyes. "Wow, Nana, you should write that down on a poster and frame it. Better yet, tell Mom to paint a little painting with those words of wisdom."

He chuckles. "Making fun of your old grandfather, eh? Where is your mother anyway?"

I shrug. "I don't know. She said something about visiting old friends." I don't mention Sohail. I have a feeling that would make them freak out.

Nani sniffs again. "What old friends? They all turned their backs on her when she married your father."

Dear Dad,

I think you probably know that Nana and Nani don't exactly like you. I wonder why. Did you ever meet them? Did you ever tell them you loved their daughter and were excited about starting a family with her? I

*wish they had the same memories of you that I do, your
deep laughter, your crinkly eyes, your musky cologne.*

*I hope I find you one day. Do you know what I'll
say if I ever stand in front of you, face-to-face, father to
daughter? Actually, I'm not sure. I may cry, although
I hope I don't. I may also get really angry and choke
up. I have a habit of doing that sometimes.*

*Do you know what my worst fear is? That I'll meet
you someday in passing, but I won't even know it's
you. And worst of all, you'll never, ever recognize me.*

> *Yours,*
> *Mimi*

Mom still hasn't come back by late afternoon, so Sakina and I go for a drive again. We roam an outdoor clothing market, Malik trailing behind us reluctantly. I run my hands over fabric splashed with vibrant reds, cool blues, and rich purples. "Only six hundred rupees, miss," a shopkeeper calls out. My eyes widen as I do some math in my head. That's less than five dollars!

I'm fascinated by everything. How colorful, how inexpensive everything is here! The customers are a mix of rich and old, young and poor. I linger at a wooden cart with rolls of embroidered cloth stacked against one another, each a shade different from the one next to it. My fingers stroke the textured smoothness over and over. Sakina shakes her head and drags me away, but not before I take a few pictures of her among the fabric backdrops, the setting sun giving off its own beautiful hues. I even get one of Malik as he stops to give a beggar woman a few coins, their faces bronzed and beaded with sweat.

We walk back to the car. The sun drops closer to the horizon in a fiery blaze, and the azaan sounds loud and clear just behind us. *Allahu akbar! Allahu akbar!* God is great! God is great!

Malik hands me the keys. "You two stay here. I'll be right back after maghrib prayer, Maryam Ji," he says, and disappears.

"Is there a mosque nearby?" I ask a shopkeeper.

He's already closing his shop and hurrying away. "Come, follow me."

I stuff my phone in my pocket and rush after him, Sakina trailing behind, muttering about being late. "Come on, slowpoke," I cry, and my voice rises up like a bird searching for freedom.

The mosque behind the market turns out to be huge, and very beautiful. The entrance is a wide archway with blue-green tiles, where the shopkeepers have left their shoes. I kick off my sandals and walk inside, then stop short with a quick breath. An expanse of tiled courtyard, yellowed by the traffic of bare feet over who-knows-how-many years, stretches out in front of me in welcome. I marvel at its coolness under my toes.

"You can't be in here." Sakina catches up to me and whispers in my ear. "Unless you're praying."

"Maybe I'm going to pray," I whisper back. I can't take my eyes off the small group of men, standing in straight lines, heads bowed, eyes closed. Malik is there, his gangly body a serene sapling waving in the breeze. They look so peaceful, so content with their lives in that still moment. "Where are the women?"

Sakina points upward, and I notice a staircase going up to a second floor, open to a second-story verandah. A few women wrapped in colorful scarves and fabrics stand in the recesses. We go up the stairs like cautious mice in a new kitchen. Sakina hesitates, then begins to pray in a corner, slightly away from the other women. I wrap my scarf around my head and follow her actions. Standing, sitting, prostrating. It's familiar and strange at the same time, as if I've done this a thousand times in a dream. *Oh God, if you're there, send Dad to me. Please. Just for a few minutes, so I can hug him one time.*

Later, Sakina and I sit cross-legged on the floor, watching the sun slide under the horizon with red streaks. "I haven't prayed in a long time," she admits softly, not looking at me.

"Why not?"

"I don't know. I just . . . find it hard to believe in God these days."

For once, I have zero questions running around in my mind. Is this what prayer does to you? Puts a sort of peace in your heart? I sigh. "You have to admit, this is very nice."

She gives a dry little laugh. "You don't even know how to pray, do you?"

"I do too!" I pause. "Well, most of it. I'm a bit rusty, like you."

"How come?"

"Nobody ever taught me. We don't go to the mosque or anything in Houston."

She considers this for a minute. "Maybe now you will?"

"Maybe." I change the subject. "How's your English practice coming along?"

She smiles. "Really good. I think I'm better than I was before." She pauses, her smile fading. "Am I? What do you think?"

"Yes, definitely better than before," I assure her.

"You're a good teacher, that's why."

I shrug. "Whatever. I'm not a good searcher, that's for sure."

She knows what I'm talking about. "Still no sign of your father?" she commiserates. "It's not your fault.

He's just good at hiding, I suspect."

I'm silent. I'm not sure if that's a compliment or an insult. "Tell me something about your father," I ask her, desperate.

"What do you want me to say, Mimi?" She puts a hand on my shoulder. "Abba is kind and generous and loving, just like other fathers. Yours must be, too, I'm very sure."

"Funny, I'm not sure about that at all."

She's silent for a while. I wait. Sometimes she takes a few minutes to collect her thoughts, and I can almost feel her translating them from Urdu to English. "Look, you have to . . . you have to trust your memories. You know he loves you. Just because you can't, eh, physically be with him doesn't mean anything. You are, how do you say, a part of him, and he's a part of you. You have to trust that."

I lean back against her, thinking. The sun is out of sight now, leaving a trail of pink and orange hues in its wake. I know it's there, waiting for tomorrow.

Dear Dad,

When I started kindergarten, I was scared. Not normal-scared like other kids, but freaked out at the thought of being by myself all day long. It was just three months after you'd left us. I remember standing in the school hallway, holding on to Mom's hand and refusing to let go, screaming until my face turned red. Mom sat me down on a bench, trying to reason with me, but I couldn't stop. I was so scared she'd leave me forever, too, just walk into her car and away from me without looking back. She hugged me a million times, and stroked my hair, and I never complained even though I hate people touching my hair. The other kids stared at me, probably thinking I was a big baby, then everyone went into their classrooms. Still I hung on to her hand. Finally, she whispered, "Just because I'm leaving doesn't mean I won't be with you, kiddo." It's silly how she always calls me that, like she's the hero in a black-and-white movie. I hiccupped and hiccupped, and she sat patiently with me until I stopped. Finally, I let go of her hand and she left.

All throughout the day, I kept hugging the memory of her to my chest, knowing she was with me.

Are you with me too, Dad? Your memory is getting awfully faint.

Mimi

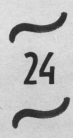

24

SAKINA
DON'T TRUST YOUR NEIGHBORS

I'm standing at the bus stop, waiting for the number 28 to arrive. The evening is silent, as if ready for something—anything—to happen. The main street near Sahib Ji's house seems to have been transformed. Every house has the flag of one political party or the other flying from its rooftop. Every boundary wall has posters of grim-faced men and prim-and-proper women pasted on it. *Vote for me! I'm the best.*

Every one except our house, of course. Our house is its usual pristine self, clipped hedges, washed walls, standing upright in the sea of jumbled election messages.

I gulp, startled at the idea that Begum Sahiba's house can be *my house*. When did that happen? When did I stop thinking of it as a prison where I had to bide my days as punishment until I'd be free? I have a feeling it's because of Mimi. Even though she's been sad lately, moping around with anxious eyes and a quivering mouth, she's got an upbeat personality that I can't get enough of. A smile that shines all the way to her eyes, especially when she's about to make one of her corny jokes that I usually don't understand fully.

I'd never tell her that, though. That would be . . . weird.

"Lost in your thoughts as usual, eh, girly?" A familiar voice grates on me, and I turn sideways. Tahira is standing next to me, grinning knowingly.

I nod at her and turn back to my position. Several other people—all servants from the looks of their clothes—are approaching the bus stop and I don't want to lose my place talking to Tahira. She shuffles closer to me. "Where's your abba's motorcycle, then, girl?" she asks loudly. A few people turn to look at me. In the land of bus travelers, motorcyclists are evil. They weave in and out of traffic, going too fast, spraying dust on passersby, often causing accidents.

Not my abba, though. He drives very carefully, sometimes making me impatient. But the damage has been done. The scowls of the other passengers are deadly. "Abba wasn't feeling too well," I admit, squashing my worry. "He left early."

"He's not been feeling well for a long time," she muses. "Have you taken him to a doctor?"

I want to stop this conversation right here. I try ignoring her, craning my neck to see if the bus is rumbling our way yet. No bus. Only a sea of hopeful passengers. "Has he seen a doctor?" she asks again. "My uncle died because we didn't take him to a doctor in time."

I turn again and glare at her. "Did he have diabetes like my abba?" I ask fiercely, my heart thumping, not wanting to hear the answer.

She smiles, her missing tooth taunting me. "Oh no, he had some heart condition. Or maybe it was something with his lungs. I don't know. Still, you should take your abba to a doctor."

With a screech of brakes, the number 28 rumbles up to the bus stop and the mass of people on the sidewalk moves forward like the tide to enter it. I struggle my way inside, pushing and pulling just like everyone else. Behind me, Tahira calls out loudly: "If you need the name of a good doctor, let me know. There's a guy in my neighborhood. He's very cheap."

Abba is sleeping when I get home. "His sugar level was very high," Amma tells me in the verandah, her face creased with worry. "Did he eat something he shouldn't have at the house?"

I'm immediately defensive. "No, of course not!" I say. "I make sure he only eats the food I take with me." But a niggling fear pushes at my forehead. What does he eat when I'm not around, when I'm out sightseeing with Mimi or chatting with her in her bedroom? There are too many temptations in Begum Sahiba's house: mangoes, jam crackers, even sugar in tea.

"Maybe we should take him to a doctor again," Amma says, and I stay silent. The doctor will ask for money we don't have, and we both know this.

She walks back to the kitchen area, where dinner is bubbling on the stove. I take a plate from the rack of dishes. The fragrance of potato curry fills my nostrils, and I can tell without looking inside the pot that it's been cooked without meat. We can't afford meat, so we make do with the vegetable versions of curry dishes. Amma does a wonderful job, though. If you close your eyes while eating, you can't even tell that it's only a few measly potatoes and green chilies.

She sits with me while I eat, both of us cross-legged on the floor near the stove. "Where's Jammy?" I ask. "It's not usually so quiet around here."

"He was making too much noise, bothering your father. So I sent him to the neighbors' to play."

Our next-door neighbors have five children ranging in age from six to twenty years old. The father works in the paper mill across town, and the mother babysits. The children are mostly all right, except for the oldest son, whose tough-looking friends hang around our street all the time. "I don't like the neighbors," I tell Amma.

She sighs. "You don't like anybody, Sakina."

I take a few bites, then a sip of lukewarm water. "Who taught me to pray, Amma?" I suddenly ask.

She looks up, startled. "Pray? I don't know. You just used to copy me in my actions every day, sitting with me on my prayer rug, mumbling the words." She suddenly smiles. "Oh, and your abba had this little book with the Arabic words of the prayers in it, and you'd look through it all the time. Even when you were little, you loved books."

"I hardly have time to read now." I can't help it, but the words come out like pieces of bitter melon.

Amma rubs a hand on my arm. "I know. You have a hard life, like all of us."

Before I can stop myself, the question comes hurtling out of my mouth. "Don't you wish you could have gone to school as a child, Amma? Don't you wish Jammy and I could?"

She looks puzzled, as if I've spoken in some foreign language. "Gone to school? It was impossible. My father was a sweeper for KMC, and my mother sewed clothes for rich women. I had seven brothers and sisters to look after. How could I have gone to school?"

My breath crushes in my chest. "And me?" I whisper, so quietly only my heart can hear.

She reaches over again and gives my arm a tight squeeze. "Come, girl, stop thinking useless thoughts. Finish your food." She turns quietly back to the stove.

After dinner, I gaze longingly at my little reading room, wanting nothing more than to crawl inside and practice my reading. Mimi has given me a worn-out book with a colorful hard cover called *Diary of a Wimpy Kid*, which I'm equal parts excited and nervous to read. She told me the words are easy and funny. I'm not so sure. The day of the admission test is looming closer, and even though Mimi thinks I'm ready, I have no such confidence in myself.

"Go get Jamshed from next door, Sakina!" Amma orders before I can take a step in the direction of my reading room.

There's no use grumbling. I wrap my dupatta tightly around my head and upper body and leave. The sky is completely dark by now, the street outside our home lighted dimly by naked bulbs on electric poles. Despite the hour—it must be nine o'clock at least—the street is full of people. Men coming home from work, their backs bent with exhaustion. Youths playing the last few minutes of cricket, yelling at one another to hurry up.

Women calling out to their children from inside their houses, telling them they've had enough play for one day. A scrawny cat limps through the garbage heap on the corner, sniffing for scraps. Its ribs are hard and thin against its muddy skin, and I turn away before I start feeling sorry for it.

Just outside the neighbors' house, their oldest son and his friends are hanging a gigantic election poster. The man's face, his large mustache, is nauseatingly familiar. Mr. Aziz from outside the *Dawn* offices! I must have been staring at him, because one of the young men calls out to me. "Hey, you! Who's your family voting for?"

I ignore him and walk slowly to the neighbors' front door, hoping to quickly slip inside. This election talk is getting out of hand. Too late. He ambles over and stands right in front of the door, hands on hips. I look at him squarely, without emotion. He's tall and gangly, with long, dirty hair that falls to his shoulders, and narrow, unkind eyes. "I asked who your family is voting for!" he repeats slowly, as if speaking to a little child.

I decide not to argue. "I'm not sure. You'll have to ask my abba." Then I realize my mistake. He's seen which house I just came out of.

He's looking behind me, a calculating expression on his face. "What's your abba's name? Is he home yet?"

"Uh, no, he's not home right now." I fumble around

for an excuse. "He's very sick. He may not even go to vote."

The boy stretches his teeth into a half smile. "We'll have to change that, won't we? Mr. Aziz is the only candidate worth voting for. I'm sure your abba will realize that soon."

"Hey, Raheem, leave that poor girl alone. She's just here to collect her brother," the neighbors' son drawls, laughing. I give him a dirty look, but Raheem steps aside and lets me pass with a flourish, so I nod my thanks in the group's general direction. There's more laughter, and Raheem saunters back to the group as if he's just out for an evening stroll.

I gather my dupatta tightly around me and walk on. This is precisely why I hate my neighbors. It's a minefield just walking outside, trying to mind my own business.

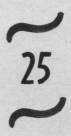

25

MIMI
A FASHION SHOW TO REMEMBER

I'm checking the calendar on Mom's laptop, and we're more than halfway through our vacation already. Some days are chock-full of activity, but others—like this afternoon—are as slow as refrigerated chocolate syrup running down a tall glass of milk. I take out my phone and find Zoe's online photo album, which she shared with me before she left. There are two dozen pictures of Italy—green countryside, little cars, courtyards full of fountains, and the occasional food picture, but none of her. She's never been into selfies all that much. I type her a text message: *Hi, how's it going?*

I wait for long minutes, but she doesn't reply. I wonder what time it is in Italy. Finally, I go back to Mom's laptop, praying to the internet gods for a good connection.

I scroll through videos on YouTube, trim my nails, organize my gel pen collection, and then watch some more videos. Cats jumping on trampolines. Little boys driving tricycles. Older boys driving bikes and failing tricks. A guy in a tank top telling knock-knock jokes. The internet connection is so slow the videos jerk and stop like breakdancing scenes, and my eyes start to ache.

"There's a cricket match on television, if you want to watch with me." Nana sticks his head in my door.

I have a very vague idea of what cricket is. "No, thanks," I say.

He insists, and two minutes later I'm downstairs in the family room watching several men amble up and down a strip of white ground with bats. I doze off, then am startled awake by a "sixer," whatever that may be. There's a lot of jubilation by one team, and a lot of head shaking and frowny faces by the other. Nana is grinning as if he made the sixer himself, so I grin along with him to make him proud of me.

"Look at us, grandfather and granddaughter, enjoying some quality time together," he says. "Your mother would be so happy to see us right now."

My grin fades. Mom's made a habit of disappearing, hinting about meeting old friends. I'm almost sure by this she means Sohail, but I haven't found the courage to ask her outright. I might miss her presence, but ever since I found those columns of Dad's, we've had this tension between us that's hard to avoid. The cricket match ends just as Sakina comes in with her usual tea and snacks, and Nana begins to read a newspaper.

"Did the match already finish?" Sakina asks, disappointed. Her eyes are glued to the television screen.

I nod. "Don't tell me you like cricket too? It's so boring!"

She gives me a stern look. "It's not boring. It's actually very exciting. I sometimes play with my brother on our verandah, but the space is tiny, and his fingers are too small to hold the bat correctly."

I change the channels on the TV, trying to find another sport, one I can actually follow. A flash of colorful fabric catches my eye. A tall woman in a magnificent purple shalwar kameez is walking down a runway. "What's this?" I whisper. Her kameez has golden sequins that should blind me, but instead completely enthrall me.

Sakina comes closer to the screen and sits down on the floor near me. "Oh, this is a fashion show. I heard about it on the radio this morning. It's very . . . how you say . . . glamorous."

I pat her on the shoulder to praise her on the very appropriate choice of words. The woman's clothes are indeed glamorous. Then another woman, even more beautiful than the first one, walks up the runway, and I sigh loudly. She's wearing a gold and silver gharara, and her lace dupatta has tassels that chime when she moves. Oh, the beauty, the rich colors!

"I think those are brides," Sakina whispers.

"You may be right," I reply. "Who else would wear such fantastic clothes?"

"My amma says they cost more than an entire year's salary," she says in awe.

"My mom could never make that much in just one year," I admit. "I wish we were rich; I'd spend all my money on these clothes."

She makes a noise in her throat, as if she's choking. "But why? None of them have any funny sayings on the front. Not even unfunny ones."

I don't tell her that *unfunny* isn't a real word. At least I don't think it is. "I will make an exception for these beauties," I tell her. "Now if we only had somewhere to wear them!"

I stand up so suddenly my head spins. Making a pose, I strut on the carpet next to Nana's chess table. I hold my head high and pout like the women on television. Sakina covers her mouth with her hand, but her laughter is too big to be contained. "You look ridiculous," she chokes out, gasping.

I grin at her and grab her hand to pull her up.

"Come be my partner. I can't be the only one looking ridiculous!"

She laughs some more, and I stop to look at her. Her eyes are crinkled, and her cheeks are blushing with happiness. "What are you staring at? I'm definitely a more beautiful model than you!" She goes into more peals of laughter, and I join in only because it's infectious.

"You girls are going to wake up Nani, and she's always cranky if her sleep is disturbed," Nana warns without looking up from his newspaper.

"She's always cranky, period!" I say. Still, Sakina sobers up at the mention of Nani, and I have to admit my laughs dry up considerably.

"I have to go wash the dishes anyway," Sakina says reluctantly. But her lips are turned up at the corners.

I smile back. "See you later, alligator."

"Are you calling me a reptile?" She's genuinely confused. I grin and help her pick up the tray of half-eaten snacks, then carry it to the kitchen even though she protests.

Mom still isn't back by five o'clock. I want to be mad at her, ask her why she even brought me here to Pakistan if she isn't going to spend any time with me. In the pit of my stomach, though, there's a niggling worry, pinching me like a mosquito in the backyard of Nani's house.

Tahira marches up to my bedroom to tell me about a phone call. "Your mother says she's sorry to be late, but she's going to be home by dinnertime," she wheezes, expressing displeasure at this lack of motherly responsibility with a frown.

"Shukriya," I reply. I've got the old newspapers Sakina gave me spread out on my bed, and I'm pretty sure I have ink stains on my forehead from where I dozed off on top of them.

She cranes her neck to see inside. "Do you want me to clean your room, Maryam Ji? It looks very untidy."

I grit my teeth. "No, thank you. I can do it myself." I don't tell her it's weird having an adult do things for me, or that this is my private space even though technically it's Uncle Faizan's room. I just smile at her until she finally leaves, muttering about untidy girls and flighty mothers.

I go back to the old newspapers on the floor. I prefer to read them even though the internet is back. Something about the paper copies makes Dad's columns more precious. I must have read them a hundred times in the last week, rubbed a finger over his photographs countless times, wondered over and over at his choice of words. *Emulate. Democratic principles. Stemming the tide of anarchy.*

Politics seems to be his expertise. I wonder if he's ever

reported on something lighter, like the latest fashion trends. Somehow the thought of him sitting at the end of a catwalk of Pakistani models, notepad in hand, makes me laugh out loud. But it's also infuriating, because there are so many gaps to fill. There's so little I know about the man whose genes I share.

Dear Dad,

If I could ask you any question in the world, I'd ask why you wanted to be a journalist. Is that surprising? I bet you thought I'd ask why you left Mom and me. But no, that's not a polite thing to ask, is it, and anyhow, I'm afraid of the answer, so it's better left unsaid.

So here's what I'd like to know. Why did you choose journalism? Did your parents want you to be a reporter? Did something happen in your life when you were a kid that pushed you to such a choice? I've been thinking hard about what path I want for myself. An artist, like Mom? Nope, I'd be struggling to pay the bills like she does. A journalist like you? Absolutely not, because the call of the story may take me away from my family.

I like traveling, and I definitely like learning about different places, different cultures. Did you know I have a big map of the world in my closet, marking all the interesting places you've been to, according to my old friend Google? I like to imagine what it would be like to visit those places, see those cities. Mom doesn't know about the map. I've pasted it on the back of my closet, and you have to swing aside all my clothes to see it.

What else could I be? Nana used to be an engineer before he retired. That sounds super boring. Maybe I could be a cook like Sakina's dad. He seems so happy doing his job, singing under his breath, eager to see what people think of his creations. Even these days, when he seems unwell, he takes a great deal of pleasure in cooking for us.

Maybe I should take some lessons from him. It will be nice to stand next to a man and learn the ropes, even if he's not my dad.

Mimi

When Mom finally comes home, she makes a pretty big announcement. "I'll be working at a children's center for a while," she says casually while we eat dinner. Today it's spinach with goat meat, potato cutlets, and spaghetti with meat sauce.

"You got a job?" Nani repeats, her voice high. "You didn't come here to work; you came here to visit us!"

I agree in my heart, but nobody's asking my opinion. As usual. Mom jabs at her plate with a fork. "It's not a real job, Ammi. I have a new job now in Houston, which I'm starting when I get back. This is a volunteer position teaching art to orphan kids. Only three times a week."

"Orphans?" Nani's anger goes up a notch. She bangs a hand on the table, rattling the china. "Not even a private school with the children of respectable parents! An orphanage! What will people say?"

I can tell Mom's gritting her teeth by the way her jaw squares and hardens. "This is why I didn't want to tell you before. I've actually been teaching the class for almost two weeks now, but I knew you'd get upset if I told you."

I look down at my food. Nobody cares that I could be upset at my mom doing something without telling me. Not just upset, but angry. Furious. Bone-tingling mad.

Nani takes desperate gulps of her water. "Two weeks? Without consulting us?"

Mom turns to Nana in exasperation. "Abba, please help?"

Nana eats his cutlets with a serene look on his face, as if volunteering at an orphanage is nothing out of the ordinary. Which it isn't, I remind myself. Nani has a habit of freaking out over everything.

"You worry too much, dear," Nana chides. "Samia is an adult. She can do whatever she wants."

"Thank you, Abba." Mom relaxes and takes a sip of Coke. But she's still hiding something, I can tell. She looks down into her glass as she continues. "There's one more thing. The orphanage is run by my friend from college, Sohail. I'd like you all to meet him. I've invited him to dinner on Tuesday."

There is a stunned little silence around the table, as if somebody pressed the pause button on a video. Then Nani gasps as if she's been slapped in the face, and Nana puts his fork down with a clatter.

I look down at my plate, but my spaghetti seems to be swimming out of focus, and I have a sudden, blinding headache.

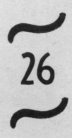

SAKINA
THE WORST DAY OF MY LIFE

"You seem tired. Are you okay?" Mimi looks at me closely.

"I'm fine," I reply, then add politely and probably unnecessarily, "Thank you for asking."

Mimi and I are practicing English in the family room, using the *Wimpy Kid* book she's given me. It's about a boy who's sad because everyone picks on him, but then he does the most obnoxious things for fun. *Pranks*, the Americans call it. I'm horrified by everything in this book, but also fascinated.

Of all the rooms in Begum Sahiba's house, I like the family room the best. It's open and airy, with large windows overlooking the back garden and the cage of mynahs. Samia Ji's painting leans against the wall in a corner, and I'm amazed at how much she's managed to complete in the few weeks she's been here. I can make out the outlines of two people sitting across from each other, heads bowed.

"Are you sure?" Mimi asks again. "You almost went to sleep practicing your verbs."

I sigh and close my notebook, where I'm jotting down words. "I'm exhausted," I admit. "Abba was not well last night at all. He just kept tossing and turning, keeping us awake."

"He should go to a doctor."

I grimace. "You sound like Tahira."

We go back to our verbs, hurriedly hiding our books when the door bangs open and Begum Sahiba strides in with an ugly look on her face. "That mother of yours, she's still not back from the orphanage?" she cries.

I gulp, but Mimi has this totally under control. She grins and waves to her grandmother. "Nani, come sit with us. Mom is always late! One time she was so late to pick me up from school they had to close all the offices and make me stand outside on the road to wait for her."

I can't tell if she's being funny or truthful. It's very hard to tell with Mimi. Her eyes are sparkling, but her smile fades when Begum Sahiba turns away to sit down. There is something bothering this girl. And her grandmother. And that something is named Sohail.

"Bring me some cool lassi, Sakina," Begum Sahiba orders. "And do it yourself; don't make your poor father work. He's not been feeling well."

I bite my lip and rush away. I can't decide which is worse, her informing me about my father's condition, or my worrying about it. I find Abba sitting at the kitchen table, breathing deeply. "Are you feeling better, Abba?" I ask, and he nods bravely.

"I think my sugar level is too low. I feel faint." I bring out yogurt and water from the fridge, mix them together with salt and sugar, and pour the lassi into three tall glasses. Abba drinks his quickly, and then leans against the back of his chair, eyes closed. "You're a good daughter," he sighs.

My throat tight, I take the other two glasses to the TV room. Begum Sahiba and Mimi are still talking about Mimi's mother. "What do you have against the orphanage, Nani?" Mimi asks innocently.

Begum Sahiba takes a long sip of the lassi. I'm expecting harsh criticism—I can never get the ratio of sugar to salt correct—but she's too worked up over the thought of her daughter rubbing shoulders with dirty orphan children. "I've been to that place. It's in a very unsafe part of the city. She hasn't lived in Karachi for so long, and she has no idea how to protect herself."

Mimi and I both digest this. "Oh, I thought it was

because . . ." Mimi's voice trails off.

"What? Because I'm a snob?" Begum Sahiba drains the rest of the lassi and hands me the glass. "I am, I suppose. But I'm also a mother, and I worry about my children."

Mimi stares at her mother's paintings in the corner. "I'm a child, and I worry about my mother," she admits in a low voice.

Begum Sahiba nods morosely. "Especially since we'll be meeting this Sohail character for dinner next week. He's sure to be very low-class."

"What's low-class?" innocent Mimi asks.

Begum Sahiba opens her mouth to answer, but I beat her to it. "Poor like me," I say quietly.

They both turn to stare, and I wait for Begum Sahiba to scold me for interrupting. She's got a strange look on her face. "I didn't mean . . ." Her voice trails off.

I take a breath to ease the tightness in my throat. Why am I upset? It's no surprise how she feels about people like me. Still, her silence is interesting. She looks almost . . . regretful?

Mimi breaks the silence with a wave of her glass. "Yum, this was awesome!" she gushes. "Can you make some more later?"

I want to tell her it's very easy to make herself when she gets home to America. Before I can open my mouth, a loud crash startles us all. "Abba!" I gasp and run toward the kitchen at full speed. The empty glass in my hand falls and shatters.

The next twenty-four hours are a nightmare I can't wake up from. Malik rushes Abba to the nearest hospital, and I ride along in the back seat, holding Abba's head in my lap. He's unconscious but breathing. I stroke his forehead every few minutes, noting how cold his skin feels under my trembling fingers.

"Don't worry, Sakina, he's just fainted because of low blood sugar," Malik consoles me in the rearview mirror. "My cousin has diabetes, and in the beginning when he was first diagnosed this happened to him a few times too."

I want to scream at him to shut up; he's not a doctor. What if my father is seriously ill and we can't afford to treat him? But I nod silently and bend over Abba. The hospital is old and dingy, with miles of patients lining the halls inside, waiting, waiting. There are other, newer hospitals closer to Begum Sahiba's house, but this one is the least expensive.

I leave Abba with an attendant and go to call Amma from the front desk. She cries on the phone but says she can't leave Jammy anywhere because the neighbors aren't home. So it's just me and Abba, together in this dreary hospital where the groans of patients who can't afford medicine fill the air and make me feel sick.

A doctor comes to see Abba. He runs some tests, orders an IV, and makes a harried examination. "Your father has diabetes," he finally tells me, as if I'm stupid.

I grit my teeth. "I know."

"Is he taking medication for it?"

I'm ashamed at the question. My shoulders slump. "No. It's too expensive."

The doctor sighs, as if it's an answer he's heard more than once. "I'm going to write out a prescription, and you have to make sure he takes these medicines. Diabetes isn't a joke, and in his case it's not something he can manage with diet alone."

I let the prescription flutter to the floor as he strides away to the next patient. I want to cry, but my eyes are so dry they hurt to fully open. I feel like smashing something, but my limbs are heavy. After a while, I pick up the prescription and put it in the pocket sewn inside my kameez. Amma may want to see it.

Amma finally arrives at night, her hair escaping from her dupatta, her face creased with worry. "The election rallies have completely blocked the main road outside the hospital," she whispers. "I've been sitting in the rickshaw for half an hour, just waiting for the traffic to let up."

The elections are so far removed from my reality right now. I tell Amma what the doctor said, and she stares at the prescription as if it's got some magic words written on it. "Maybe we can ask Begum Sahiba for a loan," she finally says, but her voice is hopeless.

Begum Sahiba. Sahib Ji. Mimi. A spark of hope stirs inside me. I rush back to the front desk to call their house, but the phone rings and rings forever. Have they all gone out for dinner, now that the cook is ill? Should I have gone back to fulfill my duties instead of being here with Abba?

Amma leaves an hour later, wanting to go back to Jammy. I spend the night lying on the floor next to Abba's bed, holding his limp hand in mine. We're in a room with nine other patients, but I don't ask what they're suffering from, nor do they offer the information. One man's head is wrapped in bandages, and another has a leg in a cast, so I suppose we're all a varied bunch of ill people and their relatives. Abba is sleeping peacefully, at least, the IV sending something healing and calming into his veins.

I try not to think about the cost of all this, but I don't sleep a wink that night. I hug the memory of the mosque in the market, sitting with Mimi as the sun sent its final blazes around us.

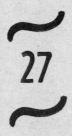

MIMI
A VISIT TO MY BEST FRIEND'S HOUSE

I stay up most of the night, thinking of Sakina's father. Is he all right? Is he at home or still at the hospital? At breakfast, Tahira is bursting with gossip. "Ejaz is going home. Sakina's mother called me on my mobile. He's doing well, but the doctor says he needs lots of medicines."

"That's wonderful news," Mom says, taking a bite of toast. "If he needs money, I can definitely help."

The thought of Sakina's family needing money is nauseating. I push away my half-eaten toast. "Mom, can I go visit Sakina? Please?"

Nani is instantly alarmed. "They live in a very dirty part of the city. No need to go there!"

I turn to glare at her. "Sakina is my friend!" I

practically shout. "I want to go see her."

Nani waves a hand at me like I'm a pesky fly in her face, and turns her attention to Mom. "See what these Americans are teaching your daughter? Servants can't be friends!"

There's a brief pause in the conversation, and I can almost hear Mom grinding her teeth in annoyance. Then she laughs a forced little laugh and tells me, "Of course you can go visit your *friend*, Mimi. The driver will take you after he drops me at the orphanage."

Nani's mouth opens and closes. "You mean you're still going to that . . . place? Even now that Ejaz is in such a terrible condition?"

Mom is already out the door. "I thought they were just servants, Ammi. Not anyone important enough to worry about."

Dear Dad,

Today another father I know is very sick. I am going to see him, but I'm more excited about seeing my friend and where she lives. Is that insensitive of me? I can't tell you how curious I am to see her house and her family, the place she calls home. She's always with me, and today I've missed her terribly.

It's funny how much I've learned about Sakina because her father is sick. Tahira told me Sakina spent the entire night with her father in the hospital. She pretends not to care about people, but inside she is so kind. She'd do anything for anyone. I know I'd do the same for you, if you were sick.

Another surprisingly caring person is Nani. She tries to act tough and shout at all the servants, but I can see she's worried about Sakina's father. She waited by the phone so long last night, cursing at Sakina for not calling to give her updates from the hospital. Nana finally told us all to get in the car for a ride to a nearby restaurant for dinner. We ate chicken tikka and paratha, but I'm sorry to report that it was not half as delicious as how Sakina's father cooks it. I can't wait for him to get well so that we can all go back to a normal diet. And so I can hear Sakina's laughter again.

Stay healthy,
Mimi

Sakina's neighborhood stinks, literally. I don't mean to be rude, and I'd never say it out loud, but the smell from the garbage piled up high on either side of the main street is overwhelmingly disgusting. I roll up the windows and breathe shallow breaths through my scarf. "Why is there so much garbage here?" I ask Malik in Urdu.

He launches into a long speech that I cannot quite

grasp. Something about uneducated people and lazy politicians. "They promise to clean up the streets, but nothing ever gets done," he mutters.

"But now there's another election coming up, right?" I ask, hoping I used the correct Urdu words.

He goes off into another speech, frowning and gesturing. The summary: elections don't change anything because the candidates are all the same. I think about this as I gaze at the posters of the different candidates plastered on the walls, all smiling innocently. One of the faces is a familiar mustached one: Mr. Aziz, the man we heard outside the *Dawn* offices earlier.

Malik glances in the rearview mirror at me. "Ejaz's house is up ahead," he points. "The green door on the right. You have to walk there—the street is too narrow for the car to pass through."

I cringe but square my shoulders. I step out of the car and walk up the street, avoiding ruts and loose rocks, even a squashed banana peel. Thank God I'm wearing sneakers. A naked toddler waves at me from his front door. I try not to stare at him, and he waves even more. The green door is just ahead of me when I hear shouting. About twenty yards away, a tall young man with long dirty hair is standing over two old men, a big stick in his hand. "You better remember what I told you," he shouts, and bangs the stick on the wall next to them. They quiver and jump. I jump with them, my heart thumping loudly.

The green door opens and Sakina peers out. "Mimi, come inside quickly!" She pulls me in and shuts the door behind us. "What are you doing here? I saw you from the window."

"I . . . came . . . to . . . see . . . you," I whisper, putting a hand on my chest to still my heart. "Who was that boy?"

"That's Raheem, the neighborhood goonda . . . I mean gangster. He's going around ordering people to vote for his candidate. Screaming, destroying things." There's an angry look on her face, mixed with a sort of desperation that comes from having your hands tied behind your back.

I glance around. I'm in a small courtyard with a sort of daybed in the front, and a kitchen area in the back. There's a door going inside, but I can't make out where it leads. It's all small enough to fit twice inside Nani's garden, with lots of space left over. A woman with long hair tied in a braid is sitting on a stool near the stove, a little boy on her lap. She stands up slowly and comes over to us, lips stretched into the gentlest smile I ever saw. The boy peeps from between her arms at me, smiling shyly. "You must be Maryam Ji," she says in Urdu. "Welcome to our house!"

"Thank you," I answer. "I . . . we . . . have all been so worried about Sakina's father. How is he?"

She looks toward the bed. For the first time I notice a shape lying there, covered with blankets. "He's much better, alhamdolillah!" the woman tells us. "Please sit, I will make us some chai."

Sakina interrupts. "Mimi doesn't drink chai, Amma."

The woman frowns. "No chai? Oh well, maybe I have some juice . . ."

I shake my head. "No, please, I don't want anything. I just wanted to meet you all."

"My dear, I cannot let a guest leave without any food or drink," she tells me gently. "It's our custom. We may be poor, but we treat our guests right."

"Okay. Juice, then, please," I reply.

"I'll leave you two friends to talk." She walks away, back to the stove, her braid waving behind her.

Sakina and I stand together in awkward silence. "I like your kameez," she finally says, pointing.

I've forgotten what I'd thrown on this morning. It's a white-and-black-striped T-shirt with a big pink donut in the middle, and the words DONUT JUDGE ME written around it in a circle. She's trying to figure it out with a tight wrinkle between her eyes. "*Do not* is spelled wrong," she tells me, concerned.

I give her a little smile. "It's a pun, with *donut*," I explain.

"I've seen pictures of donuts on billboards," she replies. "They look delicious."

"They are!" I exclaim. "And not too hard to make at home. I'll tell you the recipe."

She looks shocked. "You know how to make donuts? At home?"

"Yup. They're basically just fried batter. I told you Mom and I do a lot of cooking at home."

Sakina stares at my T-shirt some more, like it's got the answer to a puzzle hidden on it. "Yup," she repeats in a whisper.

Her mother comes back with a small glass of reddish-purple liquid. "Pomegranate juice," she says. Sakina's brother is now standing next to her, grinning proudly as if he made the juice himself. He's holding a tiny toy car in his hand.

I taste it and smile. "It's great!" I gulp it all down because it truly is delicious. Sakina's mother nods and goes back to the stove. Jamshed—Jammy—stays behind, flying the car in the air like it's an airplane. He whispers something to Sakina in Urdu, too low for me to hear.

She rolls her eyes and tells me, "He wants to show you his car. Abba gave it to him last year as an Eid gift, and he plays with it constantly."

I kneel and admire the car. It's a faded old race car with markings on the sides and a broken wheel. "Very nice," I say in Urdu.

He breaks into a smile, and repeats. "Very nice."
Then he runs back to his mother with another giggle.

Sakina gestures toward the back of the house. "Want
to see my study?"

I follow her into a sort of closet, full of old books
and papers and a few cushions to sit on. A heavy curtain hangs in the doorway, and a light hangs from the
ceiling. It's so small we both have to crawl in on our
hands and knees, and sit side by side with our arms
touching. "I love it," I announce.

She bites her lip. "Are you sure? It's so small . . ."

"So what? It's perfect," I tell her, and I'm not lying.
I can just imagine her sitting here at night, studying
for her admission test.

"I think so," she says, and we sit together quietly for
a while, listening to our breathing.

"You're so lucky, Sakina," I say after a while.

She tries to twist toward me but there isn't enough
space. "What are you talking about? You think I'm
lucky? Is this one of your jokes I don't understand?"

I shake my head. "No. You have your family with
you. You have this little space that's your own. I used
to think I was better off than you because I had more
stuff, but it's not really true. I'm not a whole person,
only half."

I can tell she's startled by my words because her body is shaking just a little bit next to mine, and her breathing is hard, as if she's been running. "If you find your father, you'll be whole again," she finally says, knowing what's in my heart.

I clamp my lips shut, and we rock back and forth together for a long time. I know without being told she's thinking of her father, asleep in the bed outside.

"How's your father doing, really?" I suddenly ask. "What did the doctor say?"

She makes a choking sound, a cross between a laugh and a sob. "He says my father needs to take some medicines to control his diabetes. The diet and exercise aren't enough."

I don't understand. "So what's the problem? Get the medicines, make him feel better."

She turns and finally looks at me, and her face is twisted into a crying, angry mass. "Easy for you to say, Miss America! Medicines cost money. Lots of money. We didn't even have enough to pay the hospital for the night we spent there. Amma had to beg the neighbors to give us money in exchange for cooking food for them for the next two months."

I digest this in silence. The tiny room—closet—seems suffocatingly small now. I want to hug the anger away from her, to make her smile that reluctant smile of hers again. I scramble out of the closet. "I'm sorry. I didn't mean to make you sad."

She sits in the closet by herself, arms wrapped around her knees, looking like a little girl. "I know," she whispers. "I just need to be alone for a while."

I put a hand in my jeans pocket and take out an envelope. "Here, take this money," I say solemnly, holding it out to her. "My mother sent it. She was going to give it to you when we left, but you need it now, I guess."

She glares at it. "No! I don't want it."

I knew she wouldn't take it easily. "You've done so much for me and my mom. You deserve it. Your abba deserves it." I put the envelope down on the floor next to her feet and turn away. "See you later, alligator."

28

SAKINA
FINDING LOST THINGS

I don't want to take the envelope Mimi's thrown so casually on the floor. Okay, she put it down carefully, but that's not the point. It sits in front of me for a long time, gleaming white against the dark stone. My study corner is like a comforting womb, surrounding me with its silent, musty, bookish smell.

I can hear Jammy playing outside with his friends, arguing about whose toy car is the best. Amma calls me for dinner, but I don't budge. She doesn't call me again. I hear Abba moving about, coughing slightly, talking to her in low tones. Slowly, the night progresses, and the envelope blinks at me as if it's alive.

Still, I keep sitting with my knees drawn up against my cheeks.

When the whole family is finally asleep, I crawl out and pick up the envelope. My hands are shaking as I open it and count the money inside. It's enough for the hospital bill and all Abba's medications for the next month. Maybe more. My legs feel weak, and I lean back against the wall. I want to throw the money away, or better yet stomp into Begum Sahiba's house tomorrow morning and throw it at Mimi's face, screaming at her to take back her charity.

But I don't. I close my fist tightly over it, keeping it safe from my own temptations.

The morning is already promising to be a hot one. I've worn the only jeans I have, paired with a long white T-shirt and tennis shoes bought last year from a second-hand thrift market. Amma frowned when she saw me going out like this. "Where are you going dressed like a begum sahiba?" I went back inside and wrapped a big white dupatta around myself to please her, but didn't tell her where I was going.

I really wasn't sure myself. Mimi's generosity the night before had kept me tossing and turning, wondering how I could ever repay the favor. How could a poor girl like me give a rich American girl like her anything of value? But just after dawn, when the sky was a blushing pink around me, and my eyelids were heavy, I realized that there *was* something I could do.

It's Sunday, so I don't have to worry about going to work at least. First, I head to the neighbors' house to repay the money for Abba's hospital bill. Raheem is standing guard outside like an angry bull, stick in hand, shouting, "Vote for Aziz, or suffer the consequences!" I want to go right up to his face and tell him that intimidating voters is illegal, and that we live in a free country where elections are supposed to be fair, but his stick worries me. He's got the posture of a person with lots of power behind him, and suddenly the image of Mr. Aziz himself comes to my mind, smiling that cruel little smile and assuring people he is the best candidate.

The neighbor aunty who babysits Jammy opens the door and ushers me inside. "Quickly, we don't want to give that badmaash a chance to come in again."

I'm aghast at the scene in front of me. Broken chairs and tables, a cracked mirror on the wall. Clothes strewn about on the floor. "What happened?" I gasp, but I already know.

"Raheem forced his way inside just a few minutes ago! He demanded to know who we were going to vote for. My poor husband made the mistake of giving a name from the other party, and he got furious." The woman has tears in her eyes. "I'm just glad he didn't hurt anyone."

"Can't you tell the police?" I stare at the mess, almost mesmerized. Abba always tells me the police are of no use, but I can't believe they'd refuse to help once they see what I'm seeing here.

She shakes her head. "I'm too scared. Raheem might come back."

I give her a little hug. I've known this aunty since I was little, and she's always taken such good care of Jammy. Amma would never leave Jammy with anyone else. "Well, I have some good news, at least," I say. "Here's the money we owed you for Abba's hospital stay." I hand her some rupees from the envelope Mimi gave me.

She wipes her tears. "Are you sure? Where did you get this money from? I thought you'd wait until next month when you got your salary."

It's killing me to give up even one rupee of my stash. It's not every day a servant girl holds this much wealth in her hands. Still, I know what I must do. I give her one last squeeze and turn away. "We don't like being in debt," I call out as I leave.

Next stop, the *Dawn* offices. It takes me thirty minutes in a rickshaw, jolting along the roads, inhaling the fumes from the cars around me. The offices are even taller and more imposing than I remember, maybe because I'm alone this time, with no Mimi to protect me. I stand outside for a few minutes, peering through the big glass windows that line the front of the building. Men and women walk about with serious looks on their faces, some carrying briefcases, others with piles of folders in their arms.

I check my body one more time to make sure I fit the part. Inside, my stomach quakes. Here I am, pretending to be a rich, modern girl who's sure of herself. Jeans scream modern, as far as I can tell. I take deep breaths and enter the building with a toss of my head. Thankfully, the receptionist is a very young man this time, with pimples on his face, his crisp white uniform too loose for his body. "Yes?" he asks, and his tone tells me he's ready to help. Eager, even.

I've stuffed my dupatta into my bag, and it feels as if I'm naked without it. I smile as if I haven't got a care in the world, emulating the pull of Mimi's lips as much as I can. "I'm looking for Tom Scotts, special correspondent," I say in English. "I know he's in this building; I just need a floor number, please."

The young man looks around uneasily. "Er, I'm not sure you're allowed to go inside?" he says, almost like a question. He must be new; his nervousness is coming at me like waves at Clifton Beach.

I can feel the tension leave my body. "I've been there

a hundred times before," I lie quickly. "In the children's section. You know. *Dawn Kids?*" I've seen that section in the Saturday paper at Sahib Ji's house. I've even pored over its contents some afternoons. Right now, I can't remember what it's officially called, but I'm taking a chance that this young man doesn't know either. I feel almost sorry for making a fool of him.

Almost, but not quite. Mimi needs me. She needs her father. And for that reason, I'm willing to swallow my fears and even lie a little bit. The God that Abba believes in—the God I felt around me in that market-place mosque—will forgive me.

My acting is superb. The receptionist nods and turns to his computer. "No problem, miss. Let's find this Tom Scott you're looking for."

"Scotts, with an *S*," I remind him, curling my fingers into my palms so hard the nails cut into my palm. I loosen my hold a little bit. *Quickly, quickly,* I beg him in my mind.

He takes his sweet time, but finally looks up with a grin so big he might as well have found the cure for cancer. "I got it! Seventh floor, room 732."

The lifts are at the back of the hall. Mimi calls them elevators. The ride on the lift is the longest I've ever taken, although it could just be because I haven't been on too many lifts in my life. 1. 2. 3. A woman gets in on the fourth floor, barely glancing at me before going back to reading a paper in her hands. I'm feeling sick, but I squash the nausea before it can take ahold of me. 5. 6. 7. The doors slide open, and I peek out.

"Is this your floor?" the woman asks impatiently in English, and for a moment I blank out. Which floor was I supposed to be going to? My heart pounds like a drum announcing bad news, and I feel faint. I focus on the lift's buttons. "Yes," I mumble, and step out just before the doors begin to close again.

I stand perfectly still, breathing shallow breaths and telling myself to calm down. If someone asks me, I'll say I'm a servant looking for her begum sahiba. My heartbeat slows down to an almost-normal rate. The seventh floor is full of activity, with rows and rows of desks lined up in twos. People are working with their heads down, phones are ringing loudly everywhere, and there's a buzz of conversation that feels almost . . . exciting. So this is what a newsroom looks like. This is where they make the newspapers Sahib Ji reads for hours every day, that line the plates of the oily foods my abba makes.

Eventually, I remember what I'm here for. I look around. Along the side of the room are doors with numbers on them. I approach the first one. 720. I walk farther along until I get to 732. Dare I knock?

"May I help you?"

I whirl around, my heart jumping again. A tall man in black trousers and a white collared shirt open at the neck stands smiling behind me, coffee cup in his hand. I try not to stare. His skin is as pink as a newborn calf's, his hair is like fine gold thread. I tremble. This is Mimi's father, I'm sure of it. He's just like the picture in the old newspapers, down to the wrinkles around his eyes, which are the same pale color as Mimi's. "Uh . . ." I can't think of anything to say. Hadn't really considered what would happen if I'd found what I was looking for. Who I was looking for.

We stand staring at each other for several painful seconds. "*Dawn Young World* is on the third floor," he tells me, and disappears into room 732.

I swallow, willing my feet to move. Should I talk to him? What could I possibly say? *Your daughter can't stop thinking about you even though you probably don't deserve it. Do you ever think of her? Would you like to meet her? She has a thousand questions to ask you.*

But I can't. I turn around and run, back down the hallway, into the lift and down to the first floor. The pimply young man at the front desk stares at me with an open mouth, but I don't care. I keep running, and I don't stop until I'm back on the street where I belong.

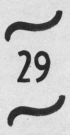

MIMI
GUESS WHO'S COMING TO DINNER

"Sorry I'm late," Sohail says in English, even though he's rung the bell at 7:02 p.m. on Tuesday evening. Has he never heard of Desi Standard Time?

I've been sent to open the front door, since Tahira is busy putting the finishing touches on our table settings. I want to bang the door shut in his face, hopefully crushing his feet in the process, but I decide that will get me in serious trouble with Mom. I shake my head and tell him, "You're not late," but I stand staring at him anyway, his smart navy blue trousers, his crisp long-sleeved gray shirt open at the collar, and the brown loafers on his feet. He looks like something out of a Pakistani magazine. Classic.

He lets me stare at him. I hope he appreciates my

T-shirt, which says *HOW MAY I IGNORE YOU TODAY?* He wiggles his eyebrows, and I realize I'm gripping the doorframe with my right hand. I let go and stand aside to allow him to enter. He smiles cheerfully, as if everything is normal, and comes all the way inside.

Nana and Nani are not in the fancy living room, the one reserved for special guests. They sit like statues on the leather sofa in the family room instead, disapproving looks on their faces. Nani does, at least. When I walk in with Sohail, she wrinkles her nose as if she's just smelled a dead rat.

Nana stands up and shakes hands with him. "Assalamu alaikum," he says. Then he clears his throat loudly. I want to giggle, but I don't think it will match the mood my T-shirt is portraying.

Sohail doesn't seem to mind. "Wa alaikum assalam," he answers easily.

Then Mom enters the room, and we all gasp. She's looking . . . beautiful. She's in a white cotton tunic with pink embroidering on the neckline over loose black pants that swish when she walks. Her hair is a wavy mass pinned on one side with a clip shaped like a pink flower, and when she passes by me, I smell strawberries.

Nani sits up even straighter. "Samia! You. Look. Very. Nice."

Immediately, the adults forget about me. I sit in the

corner near Mom's paintings, swinging my feet as the others talk around me in a mix of Urdu and English. Or at least Mom and Sohail talk. Nana joins in now and then, but Nani is mostly silent, her displeasure rolling around the room in waves. Mom smiles and laughs so much, her voice grates in my ears.

After a while, Nani apparently decides she's had enough. "So you're the administrator of that orphanage I keep hearing about," she announces, her eyes glinting.

Sohail nods. "Yes, Aunty. We have one hundred and twenty-four children anywhere from newborns to seven years old in our care. We're funded by some very big private donors, alhamdolillah."

"I thought you met Samia at university," she pounces. "Didn't you finish your education?"

"Oh, I did. I completed my MBA and then joined this organization."

There is a silence in the room I don't really understand. Nani struggles to ask, "You mean you chose to work there even with your MBA? You could be working at a bank or a multinational corporation . . ."

He nods as if it's the most natural thing in the world to be asked such personal questions. Mom's smile grows another hundred watts. "You should come by and visit the orphanage some time, Ammi. It's a very nice place."

Nani makes a choking sound.

"No pressure, of course," Sohail adds a little uneasily.

I wish I could be anywhere but here. I see Sakina peeking into the room from behind the half-shut door. Despite the elections, she and her father have stayed late to prepare dinner for us. She narrows her eyes at me and knocks on the door. "Dinner is ready," she whispers in Urdu, then runs away, her slippers flapping on the tiled floor.

Nana stands up and wags his eyebrows. "Good! I'm hungry," he announces, even though he usually doesn't eat until after the nine o'clock news. Everyone follows him, leaving me sitting alone in my chair, wishing this night would end already. If have to watch Mom toss her hair back one more time, I will puke.

Sakina comes back for me. "Aren't you coming?" she asks from the doorway. "Abba made your favorite, chicken kabab."

I keep sitting. "What's the point?"

She's too busy staring at my T-shirt. "Didn't you want to wear something nicer?" she asks, her eyebrows squished tightly together. "This guest seems to be very special."

"Shut up." I stand quickly and stomp out of the room.

Tahira has set the dining table beautifully. Big porcelain dishes with steaming-hot food, a crystal water jug, fine china plates, and the shiniest of silver cutlery.

I'm almost afraid to touch anything. The conversation flows around me. Mom talking about Houston, and her new job she's so excited about starting in the fall. Sohail reminding her of stupid college pranks they used to play on their friends. Nana telling a joke about some election candidate or the other.

I chew on my chicken kabab, dipping each bite in minty yogurt for flavor. "Would you like to try this biryani, Maryam?" Sohail asks me from across the table. "It's really delicious."

I shake my head. "No."

Mom gasps, as if I've committed a grave mistake. "Mimi, please be respectful!"

"No, thanks," I whisper.

Sohail smiles at me. "Too spicy, eh? I have to admit I prefer cheeseburgers over biryani any day."

I'm sure he's joking. Nani grunts next to me. "I suppose my cook shouldn't have bothered with all this food, then."

Sohail's smile slips a bit. "Uh . . . no, it's all very delicious," he finally replies, and it's great to see him flustered. He squares his shoulders and goes back to his food, but not before he's given me a secret wink. I stare at him with a hard face. *Getting in trouble with Nani isn't nearly enough to make me like you, buddy.*

Mom taps him on the shoulder, and he turns to her.

She's smiling with a sort of brilliance that I haven't seen in forever. I avert my eyes and smash a piece of kabab viciously on my plate. Drops of yogurt fly everywhere. "Mimi, what's wrong with you?" Nani frowns at me.

I stand so quickly my chair scrapes the floor in a sound as ugly as my feelings. "I don't want to eat anymore. Can I go?" I ask nobody in particular.

Mom wrinkles her eyebrows in a distracted way. "Sure."

Dear Dad,

Things are getting worse. Mom seems to be forgetting you, but do you even care? I once read a quote that I never quite understood. Something about a tree falling in a forest. Here's my question to you: If Mom and I forget about you, will you even exist?

Okay, you'll exist in your own life, but you won't exist for me. All I have are memories, and they're getting fainter and weaker as time goes on. I really need to find you before it's too late, but now there's a new question in my mind.

What if you don't want to be found?

M

30

SAKINA
WHAT ABOUT MIMI?

The guests are taking their time with dinner. I can hear snippets of conversation, punctuated with Samia Ji's bright laughter. I wonder what they're talking about. The guest—Sohail—is the center of attention, but not always in a good way. I've seen Mimi glowering at him several times, and I think she may be trying to put the evil eye on him.

I'm willing to bet Mimi knows nothing about the evil eye.

I pace the kitchen, eyeing my tiffin of food, but Abba says we can't eat until they've eaten. "What if they need some more salad?" he asks. "Or another bottle of Coke?"

I have only drunk Coke a handful of times in my

life and haven't been impressed. It burns my throat when I swallow it. Mimi is a Coke addict, and Begum Sahiba sends Tahira to the market every three days to get a new case of cans.

My stomach growls, and I sneak a few pieces of roti into my mouth when Abba's back is turned away from me. "What do rich people talk about?" I ask.

"What?"

"They're always talking and laughing while they eat," I explain. "Not like us. We eat our dinner quietly and quickly. But at Begum Sahiba's house they take their time, and always talk a lot. Don't they know it's dangerous to talk while eating? You could choke."

Abba checks on the pots on the counter. "Begum Sahiba and her husband have much to talk about with their daughter. Samia Ji hasn't been home for ten, twelve years. They've got a lot of catching up to do."

I shake my head. "No, it's not that. I've seen the same thing in the mall, and at fancy restaurants. And that ice-cream place we went to a few weeks ago? People were just sitting around talking. I ate quickly so my ice cream wouldn't melt."

Abba sighs. "Sakina, since when have you started asking so many questions? You sound just like Maryam Ji."

"Mimi," I automatically correct. It's been a long

time since I've thought of her as Maryam Ji. Mimi is friendlier, less formal. It somehow lessens the distance between us.

"Rich people have fewer worries, I suppose," Abba walks toward me, stumbling slightly. "You and I are made silent by our troubles."

I look at him closely. He's very pale and sweat trickles down his forehead in a reminder that he's not well. I kick myself mentally for not getting his medicine yet. I have to go all the way down to the big hospital pharmacy to get it, and I haven't found time yet. I'm a terrible daughter. "Sit down, Abba," I tell him, dragging him to a chair at the kitchen table.

He sits down heavily. "Get me a glass of sugar water," he whispers. "I'm feeling faint."

That will take too long. I grab a can of Coke and pour it into a glass for him, spilling a few drops in my haste. "That means your blood sugar is low. The doctor says it happens a lot in the early days of a diabetes diagnosis. You'll learn to manage it better, inshallah." I hope I'm looking confident, not guilty.

"Look at my daughter, so knowledgeable." He smiles a kind smile that makes my lips curve upward all on their own. He takes the glass and drinks up, making a bitter face as the Coke hits his throat. I wait for him to scold me for opening one of Mimi's cans, but he just sighs and rests his head against the chair's back.

I reach over and push the roti toward him. "You need to eat food, Abba. Tahira is in the dining room in case they need anything."

Abba eats in silence. I watch him like a hawk over its little ones. "Stop staring at me. You're going to give me indigestion," he finally complains.

A little laugh escapes me. "Sorry."

He motions to the chair next to him. "Sit down, girl. You're making me dizzy, standing over me like that."

I sit down and take the piece of roti he's offering. It tastes bland and dry without any curry, but I'm used to eating it like that. "Inshallah, I'll get your new medications very soon," I promise, thinking of Mimi's envelope. "A special injection that will make you feel much better."

He chews slowly, eyes closed. "Forget it, my darling. Those things cost more than a raja's crown. We can't afford it."

"Maybe we can," I say slowly. "Samia Ji gave us some money . . ."

He shakes his head without opening his eyes. His voice is weary. "It doesn't matter. No gift is continuous. Samia Ji will leave soon, and we will still be poor."

I'm glad I already swallowed my roti, or I'd have choked on it. I slam my hand down on the table. "So what, then? You should just keep getting sicker and sicker?"

His eyes fly open and he puts up a warning finger. "Don't be rude, daughter. We shouldn't get angry about things we cannot control."

I sigh, deflated. "How can you be so . . . calm?"

"With age comes wisdom," he replies with a little smile. "You like to act like a grown-up old lady, but you are just a girl. Remember that."

I almost stick out my tongue at him like Mimi does but stop myself in time. I make do with wiggling my eyebrows. "Just a girl who's wise beyond her years, eh?"

He chuckles, and I'm happy to see the color come back in his cheeks.

Tahira bustles in with an empty dish. "Everyone loves the biryani," she remarks loudly.

"Why wouldn't they?" I demand. "My abba makes the best biryani in the city."

"Well, I don't think it's that great," Tahira replies. She begins ladling more biryani on the empty dish, and I have to bite my lips before I tell her to leave some for me. I have my tiffin, don't I? I have no need for rich people's food.

"So tell me about this mysterious guest." Abba changes the subject before we get into an argument. "Someone else interested in marrying Samia Ji?"

Tahira stops ladling and comes over to sit with us. "What a handsome young man," she marvels. "And he's not a rich kid either. Works at an orphanage, for God's sake."

"Well, everybody doesn't like him," I say, still mad about the biryani. "Begum Sahiba's frown is so huge it's practically covering her entire face, and Mimi was sending him super-laser eyes before she left the table."

"What?" Tahira and Abba both turn to me in confusion. "What are super-laser eyes?"

"Nothing," I mutter. Mimi and I watched a super-hero show the other day, where the villain destroyed entire cities with his red laser eyes. I don't think Abba would be pleased.

Tahira stands up with the dish of biryani. "Poor Mimi. It has to hurt to have a new man trying to win her mother's affection. In the old days, nobody paid a bit of attention to divorced women. I suppose things are changing."

Abba finishes off the last of his roti. "That's good," he says. "Samia Ji is a lovely person. She deserves some happiness."

I can't stand it anymore. "What about Mimi? Doesn't she deserve to be happy? To get to know her real father?"

Abba looks perplexed. "Well, of course. But only Allah knows where he is."

Tahira is almost out the kitchen door. She looks back one last time. "I heard he's dead."

I want to throw something at her. Tom Scotts isn't dead, and all of a sudden I have an uncontrollable urge to shout out that I know exactly where he is. Then I remind myself that Mimi is only a visitor here. Soon she'll leave and go back to her beloved America, and I'll still be stuck with very real problems, like a sick father, an overworked mother, and an English test looming like my worst enemy.

I grab a can of Coke and gulp it down like bitter medicine, ignoring Abba's shocked expression.

31

MIMI
IT'S NOT OVER UNTIL I SAY SO

I sit on the steps of the back porch off the kitchen, my journal in my lap, counting the stars. The moon is full and round, bursting with light. I hear a movement behind me. "So this is where you've been hiding." It's Mom, her smile gone and her hair bundled up into a messy ponytail.

"What do you care?" I grunt.

She sits down next to me. "I care because I didn't raise you to be disrespectful," she says sharply.

I swallow. I thought she'd come to apologize, tell me she wasn't interested in Sohail, and that we could go back to the way things were before we came to Pakistan. "I wasn't being disrespectful," I insist.

"Sweetheart, everything from your T-shirt to your

silence at dinner screamed disrespect. You should have worn one of the new shalwar kameez I bought for you at the mall."

I don't want to think of the wonderful time we had shopping together. It seems like a year ago. "The new clothes itch," I grumble, even though they don't. Not much, anyway.

She sighs. "You shouldn't have—"

"You shouldn't have asked Sohail to dinner," I interrupt in a hard voice. "You should be out looking for Dad, like I am. You should be trying to convince him to come home. Not running around teaching painting to a bunch of kids."

There's a shocked silence. "Looking for your dad?" she whispers. "Why would I do that?"

I can't believe how dense she's being. "Because he's here! In Karachi!"

She's got a look on her face so harsh I can hardly recognize her. "Mimi, for the last time. He left us. He. Left. Us. Why would I go chasing after him? Why would I ever want to find him, for God's sake?"

My throat is tight. I try to speak but it comes out in a muffled sound, a cross between a moan and a sob. I don't even know how to answer this question. "For me," I whisper so low I think maybe I didn't speak at all. "Because I need him."

All the air inside her deflates, and her back curves inward. She puts a shaky arm around my shoulders. "I'm so sorry, Mimi. I can't. It's over between me and Tom. It has been for a very long time."

My sadness grows and grows until it turns into something hideous. I shake off her arm and rush to my feet in a quick, violent movement that makes me dizzy. "No!" I shout, standing over her. I'm holding my journal in my hand, and I wave it like a sword. "No, you don't mean that! You don't!"

Then, because I know she does—the set of her jaw is exactly the same as mine when I look in the mirror—I take my journal and hurl it across the backyard. Across the grass that's dark and glistening in the moonlight. Into the shrubs, away from me.

32

SAKINA
SECRETS

Abba drives his motorcycle like an old man tonight, hugging the sidewalks and stopping at every single traffic light before it turns red. I worry that we'll get stuck behind one of those noisy election rallies, but the roads are clear.

As soon as we reach home, Abba collapses in his bed. I can hear him groaning just a bit, even though he's trying to be brave. "The doctor said you need regular insulin injections," I remind him as I hang up my scarf and wash my hands with soap.

At my wretched tone, Jammy looks up in surprise from his toys—wooden spoons and an old pot. I lower my voice and sit by Abba so our conversation is more private. I've been thinking about his illness for the last few weeks almost constantly, and the worry's been increasing until it's squeezing my chest tightly.

Abba looks at me, annoyed. "Didn't we have this discussion today already?" he asks. "We can't afford the injections, so stop talking about them. It's bad enough that we had to take Samia Ji's money. We're not going to take any more charity from anyone, do you hear?"

His tone is angry, but his face is haggard, almost ashamed. I reach down and hug him fiercely. "Not to worry—I don't like taking charity either. I'll do some extra chores at Begum Sahiba's house. She said she wanted her silver jewelry polished someday."

He closes his eyes for a brief second. "This is not the life I wanted for you, my daughter," he finally whispers, sighing. "I had always hoped you'd study and make something of your life. Better than your old man, at least."

I'm stunned. He's never said this before. Before I can answer, Amma comes to gather Jammy up for dinner. "Sakina, stop chatting and make some chai for your father," she scolds. "I can't do everything on my own, you know."

I want to shout that neither can I, but it's not really an option. Like Abba said, why get angry about things you cannot change?

Amma fusses over him, smooths out his blanket. "I'm

going to telephone Begum Sahiba tomorrow," she says grimly. "You need a break from work for a few days. Sakina is more than capable of managing the kitchen on her own."

Abba grunts, but he doesn't say no. My heart sinks even more. There is no way on earth this family can survive without me.

When Amma comes back to the stove, I'm ready with Mimi's envelope. "What's this?" she asks, surprised.

I push the envelope toward her fiercely. "Can you please go to the hospital tomorrow and get Abba's insulin injections like the doctor told us to?" I whisper.

She twists her head to look at Abba, then back to face me. "Where did you get this money?"

I'm too exhausted to answer her questions. Her face is a mixture of suspicion and hope, and it breaks my heart. "Mimi gave it to me when she visited," I finally reply, then turn away to make tea.

I can feel Amma standing next to me for long minutes. Then Jammy shouts for her, and she walks away, saying, "Mimi and her mother are angels of God."

I think about this as I sit by the stove, watching the water start to boil. Angels of God? I'm not sure I believe that, but getting my hands on this much money definitely counts as a miracle. After Sohail went home today, I listened out the kitchen window to Mimi and her mother arguing. Most days I tell myself I'm better off than Mimi, despite her riches. Who wants to live in a strange land, away from one's own people? Who wants to live without a father? But most days I'm just fooling myself. Every time I see her sprawl on her bed reading, or laugh with Sahib Ji over a game of chess, I feel a strange burning in my throat.

I know what it is, but I refuse to name it.

After everyone has gone to sleep, I crawl into my study space and pick up the cookbook. It's ancient and yellowing, but the cooking instructions have been helpful in developing my vocabulary. I read for only a few minutes before I start to doze.

I'm standing in front of New Haven School, its big metal gates open for the first time. That's how I know I'm dreaming. Those gates have always been tightly closed for me; a guard in brown camouflage overalls and a long shiny mustache stops anyone who wishes to enter. He has smiles for the students and parents, but for me he's always got a disdainful half glance full of warning mixed with incredulity that I dare to consider entering.

But today the gates are open and he's not guarding the entrance. So this is definitely a dream. I walk slowly inside, flitting from the pavement to the lawn, then down to a playground with shiny metal swings and monkey bars. I reach the offices, where I've been a few times before, once to get information for my admission test, another time to actually take the test. Even in my dream I remember that feeling. Pride that I'm sitting at a small wooden desk reserved for children who study instead of working; worry that I'll fail miserably.

I sit down at a desk and work on the test. Only I can't because it's jumbled, and the words swim all over the page. I feel hot and sick to my stomach. I throw the paper on the floor in frustration and put my head on my arms. There's a movement behind me, and I turn. A crowd of people—children, adults—hovers over me, chanting, "Get out, you don't belong here. Get out, get out, get out."

I run outside, and they all chase me, still chanting. The gates are closed now, but I climb over them and fall to the ground on the other side. I look up. Amma and Abba stand in front of me with arms folded and big angry scowls. "I'm disappointed in you, my daughter," Abba says, and he's got tears in his eyes.

And then I wake up with a start.

Jealousy. That's what I feel for Mimi sometimes. For all the ways her life is easy, and mine is not. There, I named it.

I wipe the wetness from my eyes. My bag is lying

on the floor and I reach inside. I should study some English verbs; they are my weakness, and I have only a few days left before the test. I should practice my accent, make it sound more high-class. I should read *Diary of a Wimpy Kid* all over again, just to make sure I remember all the idioms and slang. *Kidding* is joking. *Dude* means person, usually a male. They say *sidewalk* in American English, but *footpath* in British. If that's on the admission test, I have to use the British word.

But I don't open the *Wimpy Kid* book. Instead, I draw out something soft and gray from my bag and open it. Despite my best intentions, I begin to read, telling myself it's practice for my test.

Dear Dad,

I am your daughter, and I have some questions for you . . .

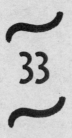

MIMI
EVEN VILLAINS AREN'T ALL BAD

The atmosphere inside Nana's house has been frigid since last night. I'm still boiling over about Mom and Sohail, and Mom's been going around with a quietly upset look. I'm secretly glad, but also secretly sad. "You should have seen Mom at dinner yesterday," I confide in Sakina. "I don't remember her ever smiling so much." We're sitting cross-legged in the living room after lunch, playing cards spread out in front of us. I've been teaching Sakina to play snap, because that's the only game I know.

"She likes Sohail," Sakina agrees, and I frown because I don't need any reminding.

"I got really mad at her last night." I launch into an account of the evening, from the moment Sohail stepped into the house to Nani's glares and pointed questions, and Nana's uncomfortable jokes.

Sakina looks distracted. She keeps looking out the window at the shrubs in the backyard. "Are you even listening to me?" I finally ask. "What's the matter with you?"

"Nothing," she mutters. "Just worried about my English test."

I don't want to admit that I'd forgotten all about it. I make an interested face and turn toward her. "When is it again? Soon?"

Sakina gives me a dry look. "Friday. Two more days."

I pick up all the cards and shuffle them. "You'll do great! Your English has improved so much since I first met you."

I mean it as a compliment, but Sakina's face darkens for a moment. "Maybe," she finally murmurs, staring at my hands.

We play for a few minutes, or at least I try to explain the rules of snap, but she keeps looking around, not paying attention. The door slams open and Mom comes in. "Sorry," she says very politely when she sees us. "I need to paint here; is that okay?"

I shrug. "Whatever."

Mom looks like she's about to say something, but she stops. She goes over to her canvas in the corner and sits down. She makes a bunch of unnecessary noises as she gets things ready for her session. "You're not teaching at your precious orphanage today?" I blurt out.

She grips her paintbrush tightly. "Not today. I only teach three times a week—it's not the end of the world."

"Whatever," I say again, and shuffle the cards so quickly they fly all over the floor in front of us.

Sakina gives me a puzzled look and starts to collect the cards. She clears her throat and addresses Mom. "Samia Ji, my parents send you their thanks. You know, for the money you sent us."

Mom smiles warmly at Sakina. "That's perfectly all right, dear. We should all help each other, whether it's through money or time."

I make an angry sound in my throat. Obviously that last sentence is a dig at me, as if I'm a villain who's stopping her from working at an orphanage.

Mom throws me a withering look and says, "Nani is going to the market with Malik, in case you want to go with her."

The thought of sitting in a car with Nani is distasteful, but it's definitely better than spending time with Mom right now. Every time I look at her face, I think of how she said, *It's over between me and Tom*, as if it's no big deal. Not even caring that it's a big deal to me. I jump up and pull Sakina with me. "Come on, Sakina, let's go."

Sakina stands still. "I have to cook today," she mutters. "Abba isn't here."

I make a pouting face at her. "Pretty please? You made so much for lunch; I'm positive we have tons of leftovers."

She inspects my face carefully. "What is so pretty about your please?" she asks. I pull her out of the room before she has time to protest anymore.

Malik is waiting by the car. "I can't take you sightseeing today, Maryam Ji," he apologizes. "Your nani has to go to the market."

"We're going with her," I announce, and climb into the back seat. Nani is already sitting there, reading something on her phone way too close to her face. She starts when I slide in first, followed by Sakina on the far end. "How wonderful," she says dryly, and goes back to her phone.

I can't tell if she's being sarcastic.

The drive is slow, with frequent stops thanks to heavy traffic. It's been several days since I went out, and I'm surprised at the tons of flags and posters on every wall. On some buildings I can't find even an inch of empty space. "Don't they have rules against this sort of thing?" I ask.

"Not everyone is as rule-loving as you Americans, my dear," Nani replies. She's put her phone inside her gigantic purse and is staring out the window.

Sakina snorts a tiny laugh, and I look at her in surprise. She's never in agreement with Nani.

Nani leans forward and looks at Sakina as well. "We Pakistanis are rule-breakers, you might say, eh, Sakina?"

Sakina snorts again. I kick her leg with mine, and she kicks back, but softly.

I hear familiar loud music in the distance. The car comes to a halt as we wait for a long line of buses with loudspeakers and men hanging off the top like circus acrobats. "DON'T FORGET TO VOTE! VOTING IS YOUR RIGHT AS A PAKISTANI. AUGUST FIRST . . . REMEMBER TO VOTE!"

Sakina sighs. "I'll be so happy when this election is over."

Nani nods and utters a tired "Mm-hmm." Then she adds, "You know, Sakina, when I was younger, we didn't have any elections at all. Pakistan has been ruled by several dictators over the years."

"That sounds lovely," Sakina mutters. "The no elections part, I mean."

I have to protest. "Come on, who'd want to be ruled by a dictator? Don't you want your freedom?"

Sakina gives me a hard look. "There's no freedom for

poor people," she says, then looks at Nani and bites her lip.

Nani nods. "It's okay, dear. I know what you mean. Money gives you freedom in some ways, but to be truly free you need other things. Good friends. Family. Your children around you. You'll learn this as you grow older."

I gulp, thinking back to my first day in Pakistan. We entered the house, and she swished into the room in a gorgeous sari, hugging us tight. It was Mom who kept her distance, who commented about the fancy house and rich furnishings. Mom who lives thousands of miles away. Funny how I'm suddenly seeing Mom in a whole new light, and it's not a great look. "Do you wish we lived close to you all the time?" I ask. "And Uncle Faizan too?"

Nani closes her eyes for a second. Her lips are twisted as if she's eaten something sour and unpleasant. "At least your mother calls us every week. Your uncle Faizan doesn't believe in phones, apparently. Everything is Facebook this and Snapchat that. He sends an email to your nana once in a while, saying he's too busy with studies and whatnot. If I didn't have Facebook, I'd have forgotten what my own son looks like."

Sakina and I exchange glances. Is she suddenly grateful for her little family, whatever problems they may have? She may be poor, but at least everyone's together. Her face is smooth and expressionless. I can't tell what she's thinking.

I want to fly to England and smack this uncle of mine on the head. Would it be too much to call home once in a while? I steal a peek at Nani as she stares out the window. I should talk to Mom about this. She always knows what to do.

Then I remember that I'm mad at Mom. That Mom hardly ever mentions her own family. Mom has too many secrets of her own. Besides, if she doesn't care about Dad leaving us, why would she care about a younger brother who always annoyed her?

I realize that the music outside is getting fainter. Finally, the procession passes by and our car starts to move again. We travel in silence the rest of the way, all three of us lost in our own thoughts.

SAKINA
THE REAL TEST

It's all like my dream from a few days ago. The big metal gates to New Haven School have been opened wide, and the guard stands by with something almost like a smile on his grim face. Only this time, I'm not alone. There is a string of students just like me wanting to take the test. A few I've seen before, when I took the test the first time, and it relieves me to know that others also failed some portion.

I'm the only person without parents here. Even the boy next to me, whose darkened face and torn kameez says he's poor like me, has an old man standing proudly with him, ruffling his hair. I turn away from their happy faces, wanting this to be over soon. I've told Begum Sahiba that Abba needs me at home, and I'll come into work later than usual. Begum Sahiba agreed without comment, which made me feel even more guilty. All the lies are making me so tired I can hardly stand straight with their burden.

The guard looks at his watch and motions us forward at exactly eight o'clock. We take the test in an empty classroom, and I can't stop looking around as the teacher—a woman with stylish short hair and rings on her fingers—passes the papers. There are big posters on the wall with smiling children and gigantic, color-ful letters in English and Urdu. A bookshelf bursting with books. A world map on the back wall, so big I can actually read the names of the cities. I search for Houston, where Mimi lives, and realize it's close to an ocean. Just like Karachi.

I think of the time I took Mimi to Clifton Beach and made her climb on a camel. She screeched loudly when the camel lurched forward, and I laughed at her. I wonder if they have camels on the beach near Houston. Probably not, judging by the number of pictures Mimi had excitedly taken with her silver phone.

The teacher calls out, "You can begin working now," and I tear my eyes away from the map. My desk is all the way at the back of the room, away from the pedestal fan, but I'm not worried. Begum Sahiba's kitchen is much hotter, and I'm not one to let a little heat defeat me. I wrap my dupatta around my head, say a quick little prayer underneath my breath, and begin.

I've finished the test early, so I decide to stop at the *Dawn* offices on my way to Begum Sahiba's house. The loud roar of the rickshaw matches the *thumpity-thump* of my heartbeat all the way here. This trip doesn't seem to get any easier with time. My tongue, gripped between my teeth, has a bitter taste. I hate lying, but it seems as if all I've been doing recently is lying. To my family, to my employers, and now to my friend.

Mimi will be gone soon, back to America where she belongs. At least she won't leave Pakistan without getting some answers to her innumerable questions.

I stand in the parking lot, clutching my bag under my arm. I don't want to face the receptionist again or answer any more questions about what I'm doing in a place I don't belong. Thankfully, with the elections only three days away, the building is crawling with people: reporters on important news stories, men and women going to meetings. On the far corner of the parking lot, there's a school bus with a crowd of children gathered around it. A field trip? An outing?

The children are laughing and talking, their white uniforms crisp despite the blasting heat. Two teachers herd them toward the building, shouting desperately,

"Stay together! Please stay together!" I slip inside with them, looking downward to avoid even accidental eye contact. A lesson I learned a long time ago: don't make eye contact with rich people: that's when they notice you.

The group moves forward like a pack of goats, their excited voices echoing in the lobby. The receptionist comes forward to meet them; it's Rubina, the woman with the hot pink nails and arched eyebrows Mimi and I met the first time we came here. There's no way I want her to see me.

I begin to panic, but she's not even looking at me. Her smile is replaced with a frown, and she's holding out her arms wide as if to gather all the schoolchildren to her. I grab my chance. I slip away from the back of the group and walk—not too fast—to the lifts, and jab the button repeatedly with a shaking finger. One, two, three, four, five . . . The doors open and I'm inside. I wait for a yell from behind me, someone shouting "Hey, servant girl, come back!" but there's nothing except the echoes of the happy, uniformed children ready to tour a newspaper building.

The seventh floor is quiet, but room 732 is open this time. I peek in. Tom Scotts—Mimi's father—is working at his desk, head down. The room is neat—too neat. The shelves are empty and boxes sit on the floor, filled with books and other things. Is he moving to a new office? Leaving for another job?

"You again?" He looks up at me, annoyed.

"Um . . ." I open my bag and take something out with sweaty hands. "I need to give this to you."

He looks at the book I'm holding out. Mimi's journal. "What is this?"

"It's for you. From my friend . . . a girl."

"A girl?" His eyebrows come together in a scowl. "If this is for a news story, you need to go to the first floor. They take tips from the public. I only write commentaries. Well, I used to. I'm not officially working here anymore."

He stops talking, and I want to smile. Everything about him—his floppy hair, his frown, the way he talks fast then stops as if reconsidering his words—reminds me of Mimi. His light brown eyes are an exact copy of hers, or is it the other way around? I'm no longer scared or nervous or anxious about being here. I know I've done the right thing. I reach forward and place the journal on his desk. His very clean desk. "It's not a news tip. It's from a girl you used to know in America. Her name is Maryam and these are her questions. A thousand questions."

His face changes. He loses his frown and a stillness comes over him, like he's been turned to a stone statue. My nerves come crashing back, and I turn and run.

35

MIMI
YOU CAN'T RUN FROM YOUR TROUBLES

"So who do you think will win the election this time?"

"Ha! No matter who wins, it's the people who are the real winners. We haven't gotten too many chances to exercise our right to vote over the last seventy years, you know."

"Oho, that means you're supporting someone who can't possibly win! Only losers talk like that."

"Well, I'm certainly going to win this game tonight."

Sohail is back, and this time he's playing chess with Nana. Their warm laughter, deep and so unlike what I'm used to hearing, floats up to me in my bedroom. I scramble up from the floor, where I'm sitting cross-legged in front of my open suitcase, and shut the door. Slam it, almost. It doesn't make a bit of difference.

Their voices float up from the open balcony.

Nana doesn't realize what a traitor he's being. I'm the one he's supposed to play chess with. I'm the one he's supposed to be talking to about the latest outrageous election news on the television. I'm the one he's supposed to be laughing with, making memories before it's too late.

I stare at the suitcase. I figure it's time to pack even though I still have a few days left before our flight back to Houston. It seems as if time grew wings and flew away from me, laughing all the while. How I hated the idea of coming here, convinced I'd have a terrible time. And now summer vacation is almost over and things have been very . . . different . . . from my imagination.

Chess. Sakina. Even Nani.

And of course Mom. I never thought Mom and I could be anything but friends. But it's been days since we spoke more than two words to each other. She's being so stubborn. Or maybe it's me. I sigh and flop down on the carpet. Nothing makes sense anymore, least of all the fact that there's a man in the family room downstairs laughing with *my* family.

Ugh. What is he even doing here? He said he was in the neighborhood after Jummah prayers, and thought he'd stop by. Before I knew it, he was invited in by a simpering mom for chai and snacks. And now, apparently, by Nana for a game or three of chess.

I can't stand it anymore. I jump up and rummage through my bedside table for my journal. It's time to complain to the only person who doesn't mind all my questions. Dad. It takes me about two seconds to not find the journal where it should be. I look under the bed covers, then on my dressing table and inside the closet.

AAAAAAAAH! Now I remember, I hurled it into the bushes that night when I was screaming at Mom. I take deep, panicked breaths. How could I have been so careless, so stupid? That journal contains my heart, poured out in multicolored gel ink. I rush out of my room and downstairs, almost tripping on the last step but steadying myself with a hand around the banister.

"Is that you, Tahira?" Nani calls out. "Bring some more chai, will you?"

I hurtle through the kitchen, almost banging into Tahira and her ever-present tray of goodies, and out the back door into the garden. That's where I sit in the evenings, counting the stars. That's where Mom and I had a shouting match the other night. And there! That's where I threw my precious journal in a fit of rage.

I hurry to the back of the garden, pushing shrubbery out of the way. I pat the mulch with my hands, and push leaves aside with my feet, and even get down on the floor and sniff for leathery smells. Nana's birds eye me suspiciously from their cage, and I lean forward to check around them. Nope, no journal. Nothing except the petals of a few brave roses blooming despite the heat, and a big fat worm exposed from my rapid investigations. I can feel my breathing get rough, my hands get clammy. I want to scream, but the family room where Sohail and Nana are playing chess is just around the corner, and the windows are always open.

I look around frantically for an escape. My eyes fall on the big iron front gate. It's closed, but I know how to open it slowly so not a creak will sound the alarm. The walls of Nani's house are closing in on me, and I can't think straight. Before I know what I'm doing, I'm out the gate and into the street, running away from the house and the journal that's no longer there.

The street is quiet. There are several rickshaws on the far corner, the same place where Mom and I got a ride to the mall together. For a wild second I think of getting in one of those rocky rickshaws and speeding away. To what? To where? Good questions. I take a step, then stop. I don't have any money.

My heart is still beating way too fast for me to head back home. I veer back toward the other end of the street. Behind the fourth house there's a children's park, where Sakina and I sat on the swings once. It's right next to a small mosque, the one where all the servants go to pray five times a day. The one whose loudspeaker azaan wakes me up in the early mornings.

Perfectly safe.

I sit on a swing and close my eyes. Back and forth, back and forth. Letting go of all my anger is harder than I'd thought, but the rocking motion helps calm me down.

There's a park in my neighborhood in Houston, across from our apartment complex and only a short walk away. It's got a sandbox and two big plastic slides, and a row of six swings. Zoe and I used to play there after school every day in elementary school, graduating from the slides to the swings and then to the benches, sitting with our notebooks and gel pens, making drawings of the other kids playing.

We haven't gone to that park in about a year.

I take my phone out of my pocket and write a message to Zoe. *Coming back home next week. Dying to see you.* Then I delete the *dying* and write *hoping* instead. Hoping to see someone sounds way less desperate. The phone beeps in my hand. There's a new message from Mom.

Where are you? Can't find you. Please reply.

I put the phone back in my pocket and swing some more. Back and forth, back and forth.

* * *

The maghrib azaan is loud in my ears when I see a familiar figure walking toward me in the distance. Nana. He's breathing heavily as a bear. "There you are, silly girl."

"I was just coming back."

He sits down on the swing next to me. The chains creak, but they hold. "I'm not going to give you any lectures because I'm sure your mother is ready with those as soon as you get home."

I kick a pebble with my foot. "She's too busy with her new boyfriend to care."

"Sohail? Ha! He's a good boy, but terrible at chess."

We sit in silence for a few minutes, and his presence is a strong comfortable blanket around me. "Nana, I lost something very special," I finally choke out. "I can't find it anywhere."

"Hmmm. Do you mean really or metaphorically?"

A little giggle escapes me. "Very funny," I mumble, but my heart is just a tiny bit lighter than it was an hour ago. Trust Nana to clear the air.

He pats my arm on the chain. "There's no point in crying over the loss of something. I've usually found that things aren't ever lost. One just doesn't know where they are at that moment."

I think about this. It's definitely been true of Dad all along. Maybe my journal is around, but hidden from view. Maybe there is a reason behind everything that's going wrong these days. Even the pain in my heart. "Okay," I whisper. "No more running."

"Okay?" He seems surprised. "Can we go home now? Sakina is going to serve fried fish for dinner, and I don't want to miss it."

I realize that I haven't eaten anything since lunchtime. I drag myself out of the swing. Nana does the same. "Ready to face the wrath of your mother?" he jokes.

I swallow. "Ready as I'll ever be."

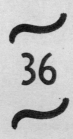

36

SAKINA
DREAMS ARE FOR FOOLS AND RICH PEOPLE

"Where did you go?" Amma stands with her hands on her hips, ready to shout at me.

I've just entered the house in the evening. My feet are hurting from the long walk from the bus stop, and my stomach feels like it's hollow. I didn't have time to eat at Begum Sahiba's house because Mimi disappeared and the whole house was in a state of panic. If they'd asked me, I'd have told them to check the park at the end of the street. But of course no one thought to ask me. I'm nobody.

Amma is blocking the door, scowling at me. I push past her and go inside. I have no time for her anger.

Why is she always angry, anyway? It's not my fault we have no money, or that Abba's diabetes is still uncontrollable. "I had to run errands for Begum Sahiba," I mutter as I head to the sink in the courtyard. It's not exactly a lie. I did make a detour to the seamstress on Faisal Road to pick up a new sari blouse. She's been reminding me about it for several days now, not caring that it's not in my job description. Still, her confessions about her son, that downcast, wrinkled face, are fresh in my mind, so I complied.

I also went back to New Haven School, just sitting on the footpath—sidewalk—for twenty minutes soaking in the atmosphere. It was evening, so the gates were tightly shut, and there was no sign of the guard who'd been there that morning when I took the test. But the school building was tall and majestic to me, the playground in sight through a metal fence, bookshelves visible through an open window of what was probably a library. I sat there for the longest time, my eyes fixed on the books, until a sort of calmness descended on me.

I wash my hands and face and find myself a piece of yesterday's roti in the kitchen. Amma follows me, her scowl gone. "I made daal; why don't you eat some?" she says, and her tone is much kinder. Softer.

I've been craving chicken, but we can't afford it. Even a few vegetables would be delicious right now. Still, I pour myself some daal and sit in the corner on a stool. "How's Abba?" I ask. "Did you get his injections?"

She sighs and sits down next to me on the floor. "Same. He's been resting." She worries her bottom lip with her teeth. "I couldn't go to the hospital yet. None of the rickshaws are willing to go there because of election rallies. And I can't take Jammy on the bus with me. He wiggles too much."

I clench my fist around my spoon. "Amma! You know this is important! Not just for Abba's health, but also because we shouldn't have money lying around the house. You know the goondas always find out."

"Yes, beta, I know. Tomorrow morning, inshallah." She sighs and pats my arm. "Tell me, is Begum Sahiba angry that your abba is missing so many days of work?"

"No, she's all right. She understands." I take a bite of roti, softening it with the daal. "I'm perfectly capable of cooking the family's food by myself, you know."

She smiles wearily. "Thank God for my daughter. What would we do without you?"

I frown and look downward, trying to hide my angry eyes from her. What would she say if I told her I'd made a second attempt at an admission test to a school? How would she react if I told her I could no longer work at Begum Sahiba's house? Who would support our family if Abba could no longer cook?

I sound like Mimi, with all her questions.

Amma's looking at me with unexpectedly sad eyes.

"I know you like to read. To study," she whispers. "I wish your father and I could have given you a different life. One where you could go to school and learn important things. One where you didn't have to work in someone's kitchen."

I gasp. Has she read my mind? I lean closer, hoping she will say more.

There's movement outside, shouting and music. Amma shakes her head and stands up. "Just five more days until election day, thank God!" she mutters. "I'm tired of all this noise in the streets."

I put my plate down, my heart speeding. "This is different, Amma."

I'm right. The shouting is more real, closer and louder. Angrier. A few people are screaming on the street outside. Abba sits up on the bed, a confused look on his face. "What's going on?"

We wait. Another minute, and our front door bangs open as if kicked in by a foot. There are four or five young men gathered in our entrance, but I recognize only one. Raheem. He strides inside as if he owns the place, and shouts, "Next week is election day; remember to vote for Aziz!"

Abba tries to stand up, but I run over to him and push him back with a warning hand. "Yes, definitely, Abba will go to the polls on Wednesday."

Raheem comes close enough for me to see the pock-marks on his skin. His white undershirt is stained yellow with sweat, and his khaki trousers are a size too big for him. A black string bracelet circles each wrist. "Good," he sneers at me. "Now let me see what money you have. Your neighbors tell me you work at a rich sahib's house, so you must have some money to share with all of us, eh?"

I gulp, my throat working up and down. "We don't have any money," I say, my voice trembling just a little bit. Amma comes to stand next to me, her arm around me like a shield.

Raheem doesn't believe me. "You want my boys to search the place?" he snarls. "Tear it down, perhaps?"

"No!" Abba croaks. He looks at me. "Give him what we have," he says.

There's no way. I grit my teeth. "I don't have anything."

Raheem looms over me until I can smell his breath. I try not to gag. "Right. Now. Unless you want someone to get hurt."

"Wait!" Amma cries. She walks with unsteady feet toward the bedroom and comes back with a small white envelope. Mimi's envelope. "Here, take this and leave us alone."

Raheem smiles a hideous smile and grabs the money. "Shukriya, Aunty!" he mocks, and turns away. "Don't forget to vote!"

All three of us stand in the same position for long moments, our bodies frozen with fear and misery. Amma sniffs, and I turn my head slightly to see tears drop from her eyes. I blink when I realize that I'm crying too. "I'm sorry," I whisper.

Abba pulls me down into his embrace. "What are you apologizing for, you silly girl? None of this is your fault."

Amma sits down besides us. "If anyone is to blame, it's me." She sniffs again. "I should have bought the injections like you told me to. I should have walked to the hospital if the rickshaw wouldn't take me."

Abba holds out his other arm to her. "Come on, Aisha. Don't start crying now. We've gone through worse."

She wipes her eyes with the edge of her dupatta. "You're right, of course. God will help us. We just have to be patient."

I can't believe they're talking like this. Patience is something I don't have. I'm tired of waiting for God. My tears come faster. I feel as if all the walls around my heart are breaking down slowly, painfully. "I don't have any more time. I need you well, Abba, so that I can stop working." Amma and Abba become still. "What do you mean, stop working?" Amma finally asks.

She doesn't sound angry, just confused. I wipe my eyes, but the tears won't stop. "I . . . I . . . applied for admission to a school. They are giving scholarships to poor children, and if I pass I can go to school. . . ." My voice trails off. I never realized what a burden this secret has been, how difficult it has been to hide this huge thing from my parents. Now that I've said the words, I feel light as a feather.

Amma and Abba exchange glances. "You want to go to school?" Abba asks softly. I can't tell if he's surprised or furious.

I hide my face in his chest. "I'm sorry, Abba, I know it's disappointing to you. You want me to be a cook like you. To work with you in Begum Sahiba's house."

His chest shakes under my cheek, and for a minute I think he's also started crying. But I hear his laughter and I look up. He's got a huge smile on his face, as if he's just heard the best news. "Silly girl, I'd like nothing better than for you to go to school. You're so smart and hardworking; you deserve to have a better life than I did."

I turn to look at Amma. She's got a worried look on her face, tinged with defeat and sadness. "Your abba is right," she finally says. "You do deserve better."

I reach out my other arm and hug her too. We sit rocking one another, listening to the shouting on the street get fainter and fainter. Nobody talks about the fact that we just lost the only money we had, and even if I do pass my English test, we can't afford to lose my income.

37

MIMI
WE MEET AT LAST

"How long are you going to stay mad at me?" Mom asks. I'm lying in my bed, trying to take the required afternoon nap. How everyone in this country just falls asleep every afternoon after lunch is beyond me. Usually I chat with Sakina, or we practice for her English test, but today is Sunday, and she's not here.

"I don't know," I reply. I sit up and rub my eyes so she thinks she disturbed my sleep.

She comes inside and sits on my bed near my feet. It's a familiar position, one she used to sit in at bedtime when I was younger. Sometime between second and third grade we stopped reading bedtime stories together. "I don't want you to be mad at me," she whispers, and I realize she's been crying. Her eyes are puffy and her hair is a mess.

I sit up too. I'm not going to feel sorry for her; I'm not. "We were supposed to be a team, Mom."

"We're still a team," she pleads. "Why would you think otherwise?"

I can't believe she can be so dense. "Teammates don't lie to each other; they don't keep secrets like knowing where one team member's dad is, or how to contact him." My fists curl into balls. I have to resist the urge to throw something at the wall or off the balcony. "Teammates share things. They tell each other about themselves and their lives."

Mom looks up. "What are you talking about? I share things with you."

"No, you don't, Mom. You never told me much about Nana and Nani all these years. You never encouraged me to talk to them on the phone or Facebook. I didn't even know your brother moved to England, or that Nani is really sad because he's gone!"

"I've just been protecting you!"

"No!" I almost shout. "You're just . . . hiding. That's it. You're hiding from everything painful in your life, not even caring that you don't have the right to keep information from other people."

She's deathly quiet. She's staring at a spot on my bedcover as if it's the most interesting thing in the world.

I see tears drop from her eyes onto my bed, but I don't move. I don't remember when I stopped being mad at her, when my anger turned to disappointment. Finally, she whispers, "When did you become so smart?"

I shake my head. I'm starting to feel the tears inside me too. "I don't care about being right. I just want things to change. You have to change, Mom. You can't pretend that everything's okay now that Dad's gone. I have a hole in my heart where he used to be, and I can't just forget that."

She takes a trembling breath. "I know. I'm sorry."

I sigh so loudly my hair ruffles on my forehead. "Stop saying you're sorry. It doesn't help."

"What will help, then?"

I get out of bed and head out the door. I need a can of Coke, or two. "I have no idea. I'll let you know when I figure it out."

The kitchen is a dark, cool sanctuary this time of the afternoon. From the window overlooking the back porch I can see Malik lying on the floor on a mat, his head covered with a piece of cloth to keep away the sun. Sakina's abba is still not back to work, but I can imagine him on the floor mat next to Malik, an arm thrown over his forehead. The two are friends, I think, which makes me happy. I can't see Tahira, so she's

277

probably sleeping on the floor in Nani's air-conditioned bedroom. Silly, gossiping Tahira, always rubbing Sakina the wrong way!

I gaze at everything carefully, trying to sear the images into my mind so I can remember them when I'm back home.

Home. Only three more days until we leave. There's a gigantic ticking countdown in my brain all the time. *Tick-tock-tick-tock.* I should be ecstatic, but all I can feel is empty, as if nothing has turned out like I was expecting.

RRRING! The doorbell. I wait for a servant to wake up, but there's no movement. Finally, I go to open the front door myself. Whoever it is, they must be brave to ring the bell this time in the afternoon. Brave or clueless.

The man standing outside is so far from my mind that it takes me a second to recognize him. Blond hair graying at the temples. Soft pink skin darkened by the Pakistani sun. He looks just like his picture in the newspaper, faded and crumpled. "Dad," I gasp faintly, and the word seems suddenly foreign. "How—what—why—how?"

He smiles, wrinkles around his eyes. "Your friend was right—you do have lots of questions."

Friend? He holds up my leather journal, and I blink.

"How did you find me?" I croak.

"There was a notepaper with this address written on it between the pages. I think maybe your friend wrote it for me? She was quite angry-looking and didn't stay long to explain."

It takes me all of two seconds to figure it out. Sakina! She must have found my journal in the backyard and gone looking for Dad all on her own. I relax a little bit, then I step outside and close the door quietly behind me. This is a moment for me alone.

Dad is looking at me with hungry eyes. "I can't believe how big you are, Mimi," he says, his voice hoarse.

I blink rapidly. I should be mad. Why aren't I mad? "Thanks. I'm eleven," I answer in a clipped voice.

He swallows sharply, and I watch his Adam's apple move up and down. "I read all your letters. I . . . I don't know what to say. I have almost no answers to all your questions." Regret and sadness are etched into his face, and without looking at myself in the mirror I know my face is the same. Same features, same color eyes, same regret and sadness.

I waver. Should I hug him? Is it appropriate to melt into the arms of a person who's practically a stranger, even if I share their genes? The thoughts buzz in my brain like a dozen angry bees. "Just tell me why you left. Did . . . did I do something wrong?"

He is immediately alarmed. He hunkers down until our eyes meet. "No! It was not you. I promise." He takes a deep, shaking breath. "Your mom and I hadn't been getting along, and then I got this really exciting assignment in Iraq, right in the middle of an insurgency. It would have killed my career not to go."

I nod, but I don't really understand. Lots of parents go away to work, but they always come back. Zoe's dad was in the air force and he spent months away from her when she was little. But he eventually came back for good when we were in fifth grade. "I guess your career is really important to you."

He closes his eyes as if I've slapped him. "I guess. After Iraq I went to Sudan, and then South Korea. Then lots of other cities and countries, even continents. I received two awards for my writing, and then I came here to Karachi."

The bees are still buzzing inside my brain, but they're contained, defeated. I don't tell him I know of every place he's ever been to. Well, almost. I hadn't known about Karachi. "Congratulations," I say quietly.

He doesn't say anything. I sink down on the steps and stare at the dirt on my shoes. After a minute, he sits down next to me. "So, tell me about yourself. The brief version, like a journalist would tell it."

I gulp. Somehow I don't recall much about myself at

the moment. "Maryam Scotts, age eleven years three months, going into Kennedy Middle School in Houston, Texas, soon. Favorite subject, geography. Least favorite subject, art. Best friend's name, Zoe Kim, currently in Italy with her parents. One mom, named Samia, and one dad, you. Grandparents who are possibly weird, but growing on me." I pause. "And one best friend here. Sakina Ejaz."

He gives a little laugh. "Good. I'm glad you have a best friend here. This Sakina looked like she cares about you a lot."

I don't have to think about this one. "Yeah, she does. She's a great cook, but the thing she really wants to do is go to school."

He smiles a little. "And what about you? What do you like to do in your free time?"

I shrug. "Watch YouTube videos. Read books. Write in my journal . . ." My voice trails off.

He says quietly, "I'm happy I got to read your journal, at least. You're a great writer."

I shrug again. I don't feel like a great anything at the moment. "Thanks?"

"I mean it. I could tell from your letters that you're growing up to be a wonderful person."

I know he's just trying to get into my good graces. Can you really learn so much about a person from their journal? But then I think of his columns and realize I learned a lot about him by reading his words. I turn to him with a little smile. "Now your turn. What's your short version?"

He looks startled, then relaxes. "Let's see. Tom Scotts, born in Atlanta, Georgia. Moved to New York for college, then Houston, Texas, where he became proud father to a beautiful baby girl. Then . . . a lot of other countries that he doesn't remember much about. Best friend, Dave, died in the war in Iraq ten years ago. Parents, Maryann and Eric Scotts, both passed away a long time ago." He pauses and gives me a sidelong glance. "Did you know we chose your name because it was so similar to my mother's?"

A warmth fills my insides at this brand-new information. "Maryann. Maryam."

"Her nickname was Mimi," he adds, and his voice is hoarse.

He's quiet for a long time. I don't mind that. I'm having a hard time with words too. Then he continues softly, "Oh, Mimi, I want to say I'm sorry, but I don't think that will change anything."

I think about this. "Mom says if someone is really sorry, they'll change their behavior." I look up at him. "Why did you come here? Is anything going to change?"

He's quiet for a while. Then he says, "I'm leaving

Karachi right after the elections. My work is freelance, so I don't usually stay in one location too long. I got another gig a few weeks ago and was just wrapping up my apartment and waiting for some paperwork. I'll be going to New York next." He has a ghost of a grin on his face, as if he's seeking permission. "At least we'll be in the same country. Maybe we can keep in touch? Write each other real letters and call?"

My heart skips a beat, but I squash down the sudden ray of hope. "I'd like that."

He slings an arm around me, and I inhale his cologne, the same lemony fragrance that's seared into my memory. "I'd like that too," he whispers in my ear, and I can feel my anger melt away.

38

SAKINA
I AM HUMAN TOO

I've cooked mutton pulao all by myself for lunch. It's a long, difficult recipe, and I've always been nervous about it. You have to choose the right parts of the goat—usually the shoulder and leg because they are fatty—and the correct strain of rice. Basmati works best, with its long grains and fluffy texture.

Abba came back to work today, but he's supposed to take it easy. He sat at the kitchen table all morning and gave me instructions—soak the rice longer, cut the mutton bones just so, add more zeera—but after a while I tune him out and work at my own pace. *Listen to your hands as you cook*, Abba's always told me. That's all I need to know.

Begum Sahiba marvels at what a good job I've done,

and I flush with the praise. She's different today, not because it's election day, but because the American guests are leaving soon. Very soon. I don't want to think about it. The house seems to be shrouded in black, mourning the impending loss of guests who've filled these rooms with noise and laughter. The curtains are drawn, the lights dim.

"I didn't know you had learned so much already from your father, child." Begum Sahiba licks her fingers delicately and pushes her plate toward me for a second helping. "Before long, you'll be able to take over from him and run the kitchen yourself."

My face falls. I'd rather be sitting in a classroom, learning fractions and geometry. Or reading Shakespeare and Faiz Ahmad Faiz. Cooking is not my ambition, no matter how well I do it.

"What?" she asks, noticing my expression.

I shake my head and add more pulao to her plate. "Take more, please."

Mimi interrupts. "Have you ever thought maybe Sakina doesn't want to be a cook, Nani?"

Begum Sahiba frowns as if she's been presented with an impossible math problem. "What else will she do, then?"

I scowl at Mimi. Her neon green T-shirt says *I'M JUST HERE FOR THE TACOS*. She scowls back.

"Nothing, Begum Sahiba," I say loudly, and walk away from the dining room before I throw something at Mimi's head.

She is persistent. She follows me to the kitchen and demands, "Why don't you tell her that you want to go to school? Maybe she can help you. She's not the dragon you think she is."

"If you're going to come in here, you better help me clean up," I reply, picking up a load of dishes and taking them to the sink. "And you're a fine one to talk. You've got some things to say to your mother, don't you?"

She stops. "Like what?"

I give her a disbelieving look. "Like . . . the fact that you've been looking for your father. Going to the *Dawn* offices without telling anyone," I venture, not looking directly at her.

She pounces on me with a catlike grin, jabbing a finger into my chest. "So did you! You took my journal and gave it to my dad. Did you think I wouldn't find out?"

I can't tell if she's thanking me or accusing me. "Yes, you're right," I finally reply, not knowing what else to say. "So you finally met him, huh?"

She picks up the rest of the dishes and brings them to the sink. Then she leans against the wall next to me, and I see she's grinning. "Oh, Sakina, it was wonderful! I hugged him, and he felt just like I'd imagined."

I'm glad for her. She's been sad for so long. She deserves to be happy. Then I pause. "Have you told your mother?"

Her grin fades. "Noooo." But she's thinking about it, I can tell. "Okay, deal. You talk to Nani; I'll talk to my mom."

I roll my eyes at her and start washing the dishes. I have nothing to say to Begum Sahiba. My life is so different from Mimi's, so difficult. Things can't be solved as easily as she thinks they can be. "Your mother will go back to normal once you two are home again. Sohail is not going with you, is he?"

She sighs loudly. "No, he isn't, thank God!"

I flick some soapy water on her. "See, leaving will actually solve fifty percent of your problems."

She reaches over and flicks some water at me. I squeal and put an arm up to protect my eyes. We both laugh a little. "I'll miss you," she tells me.

Tahira swishes in with plates from the dining room before I can reply. "Sahib Ji wants his lunch in the TV room," she announces. "He's watching the election results."

I groan. My encounter with Raheem a few nights ago is still fresh in my mind.

Mimi straightens and picks up a plate of pulao. "I got it," she calls out as she leaves the kitchen.

"Give him some yogurt too!" I yell after her.

"I know!" she yells. "That's the best part!"

When the dishes are all washed, I go back to the dining room. Begum Sahiba is sitting at the table, eyes closed. She looks tired. "Do you need anything else, ma'am?" I ask hesitantly.

She opens her eyes, and I'm shocked to see they're wet. "Can you stop my daughter from leaving?" she whispers.

I have no idea what to say, so I shake my head. "Sorry."

She blinks, and the wetness disappears. "Oh, I'm just being silly." She takes a sip of water. "So, tell me, young lady. What would you do if you didn't spend all your time cooking?"

I curse Mimi under my breath. Begum Sahiba is looking at me, waiting for an answer. I take a deep breath and answer, "Go to school."

Her face changes. I'm expecting her to be furious, to spit fire from her breath or something, but she just sits there. She's obviously surprised, as if the idea of me going to school is so foreign she just can't wrap her head around it. "Hmmm," she finally says. "So you need money?"

I shake my head violently. "No! Not for myself. But Abba needs insulin injections so that he can keep working. And I can come help him after school too."

She closes her eyes again and puts her head against the back of her chair. "It shouldn't be a problem. I'll talk to my husband about it. We need your father to be healthy, after all."

I can't believe what I'm hearing. Could I actually not be needed here? If Abba got all his medicines, could I finally be free? I rush toward the family room to tell Mimi that she's not the only one with a long list of impossible, exciting questions.

Sahib Ji and Samia Ji sit in the family room, watching television. I gaze at them from behind the doorway. The way he smiles as he points out the latest election result on the television screen. The way she sits on a stool in front of her ever-present canvas, dabbing it with a paintbrush. All this will end tomorrow, and the house will go back to being quiet and lonely.

As I watch, Samia Ji turns the canvas around and shows it to her father. I stifle a gasp. It's a painting of him and Mimi, sitting opposite each other playing chess. The details are all there, clear as a photograph. The whiteness of the chess pieces, the dotted fabric of the chairs, the sun streaming in from the windows behind them.

Sahib Ji reaches over and hugs his daughter. Soon she'll be gone, and her painting will hang on the wall of a quiet mansion.

Maybe I'll also be gone soon, if I passed my English test. I think of that moment, how the school will send me another letter in the mail, how Amma and Abba will put on their best shalwar kameez to visit the teachers with me, how I'll get a new backpack from Lunda Bazaar, the thrift market. I imagine Abba hugging me like Sahib Ji just hugged Mimi's mother, a proud yet sad look on his face. A shiver runs through my body, and I clamp it down. Nothing is final yet, and I may have failed the test.

But in my heart, I know I've passed. I knew all the answers, thanks to a certain American girl.

39

MIMI
THE LAST DAY IS ALWAYS THE BEST

"Have you checked your closet?" Mom insists, looking at my suitcase suspiciously. "You probably left some things in there."

"Yes! I packed everything, Mom."

She looks around my room. All my stuff is gone, and the furniture is neat and bland once more. "Good," she says, but her voice is distant, as if she's thinking of something else entirely.

I sling an arm around her shoulders. Now that we're leaving, I suddenly don't want to be mad at her anymore. I want us to go back to the team we used to be. Mimi + Mom. The 2 Ms. "Are you happy to be going back tomorrow?"

She thinks about this for a second. "Yes," she finally

says. "It was a nice vacation, but I'm ready to go back to my new job. I think it will be good for us."

"What about Sohail?"

She frowns. "What about Sohail?"

I don't want her getting any ideas. "Nothing. Just asking."

She moves away from me and sits on my bed. Uncle Faizan's bed. "Listen, kiddo. I know things have been difficult between us, but I can assure you Sohail and I are just friends. I really enjoy his company, but that's it. We're going back to Houston, and he will stay here managing his wonderful orphanage."

I can't tell if she's sad. Mom has a habit of putting on a brave face when things get tough. "Maybe you two can talk on Skype," I offer.

She gives a little laugh. "How gracious of you, Mimi."

My phone beeps in my pocket. *See you soon!* It's Zoe, punctuating her message with a smiley face with heart eyes. It's her first message to me since summer break began.

"Who is that?" Mom asks.

"I suddenly have a good feeling about going back home too," I reply with a little smile. I square my shoulders and sit on the bed next to her. "I have to tell you something. Something about Dad."

Her smile slips. Her face tightens. "Mimi . . ." She sighs.

I put up my hand to stop her. "Wait. Let me talk. It's important."

She has no idea what I'm about to say. I've been hugging the secret of Dad's visit to myself all day and all night. But keeping secrets isn't my cup of tea, as Nana would say.

Sakina comes into my room before asr, holding a plastic bag in her hands. "This is for you," she says shyly. "A going-away present."

I grab the bag from her. In it, is a yellow T-shirt with a big sandwich on the front and the words *NICE TO MEAT YOU*. I unfold it and lay it against my chest. "Perfect!" I exclaim. "I'll wear it on my first day of middle school when I get back home."

"It's a bun kabab, like the one we ate that day on Clifton Beach," she reminds me.

I nod. It was the best sandwich of my life. The best day of my life.

She comes all the way inside my room. "I'll be sad to see you go."

I clear my throat, then grab her arm and pull her down on the bed. "I'm not going until tomorrow. Time for one last gossip session!" I wiggle my eyebrows. "Tell me about your test. How did it go?"

"It was good," she says, grinning. "I have a good feeling about it."

"Seems like everyone is having good feelings about the future today." I lean forward and take something out of my bedside drawer. "I got something for you too."

She looks at the journal in my hand. It's sky-blue, embossed, with a bold black stripe on the right side and the words *My Very First Journal* in silver lettering. I offer it to her, and she takes it slowly, as if she's scared. She touches the cover with careful fingers. "What will I use this for?" she says almost to herself.

"Whatever you want," I tell her happily. "You can use it to practice writing, or draw pictures." I reach up and turn the journal over. "There are a bunch of matching blue envelopes in the back, so you can write me letters like I used to in my old journal."

She bites her lip and looks down, her grin gone. Is she crying? Quickly, I take out a box from my drawer to distract her. It's a set of toy cars tied with a red bow. "This is for Jamshed," I say, and her grin is back, brighter than before.

A shout from downstairs makes us both look around, startled. Nana is shouting for us. The sky has grown dark, and my stomach is rumbling. I suddenly realize something. "It's evening already. How come you're still here?"

She holds my hand as we walk downstairs, clutching the box of cars and her blue journal under her arm as if they're her most prized possessions. "Abba thought it would be better that we spend the night, because of the election results. The streets are bound to be very crowded this time of night, no matter who wins."

"I think he just wanted us to spend more time together." I chuckle. "Your abba is a sweetheart!"

"Agreed."

At the bottom of the staircase, I hear voices from Nani's bedroom. I peek in. Mom and Nani are sitting on the bed, a photo album open between them. "How silly Faizan looks with that sailor cap on his head!" Mom says. "How old must he be, six?"

Nani laughs. "I remember that thing! It was too big for him and kept falling over his eyes! But he'd still stumble around wearing it all day long!"

I smile and walk away, joining Sakina as she stands outside the family room, holding the door open for me.

Nana is alone inside, dancing a little jig. The television screen shows a big crowd of happy people throwing streamers into the air. "We won!" Nana tells us excitedly. "The elections are over!"

"What about Mr. Aziz?" Sakina asks, anxious.

"Lost so badly, he'll be crying like a baby tonight!"

Sakina hugs me, and we hold each other like old

friends. My throat is tight, and I swallow several times. "Promise me you'll write letters to me," I whisper in her ear.

"Promise."

"How about a last chess game, Mimi?" Nana asks.

I let Sakina go with a deep sigh. "Sure, but right now I'm starving." Then I reconsider. "I mean, very, very, very hungry."

Sakina rolls her eyes, but she's smiling. "Me too."

Tahira enters promptly with a tray full of food. Sometimes I think she's always eavesdropping outside the door, because she comes in as soon as she's needed. "There's plenty of Sakina's pulao left over," she tells us. "I thought it would be a good idea to eat here tonight."

Sakina's abba follows with plates. "I'm just happy the elections are over," he says. "Now we can get back to our normal lives."

"Is your family all right, Ejaz?" Nana asks, and an image of the rude young man Raheem comes to my mind.

Sakina's abba nods. "Yes, Sahib Ji, I just called my wife, Aisha, on the phone. The neighborhood is quiet, but the men are taking turns patrolling the streets to make sure the goondas don't come back."

Sakina and I kneel on the floor in front of the coffee table and eat. The pulao is even more delicious the second time around. "I need you to give this recipe to my mom so she can cook pulao for me in Houston," I say. Then I reconsider. "On second thought, give the recipe to me. I'll try to make it myself one day."

Sakina laughs. "Ha! You better take a picture of the final result and send it to me; otherwise I won't believe you."

Nana is still watching television, but at one point during our makeshift dinner, he comes over and kisses me on the top of my head. I look up, my mouth full of rice, and grin at him. "Come eat with us, Nana!"

He eyes the food laid out in front of us. "Where are your mother and grandmother?" he asks.

I shrug. "Having a gossip session in the bedroom."

He takes a plateful of pulao and goes back to his seat in front of the screen. "That's a nice change," he murmurs in a satisfied voice.

40

SAKINA
FINAL GOODBYES

The whole family goes to the airport to drop off Mimi and Samia Ji. Malik drives the car, and Abba and I follow in a taxi with all their suitcases. Samia Ji has managed to do a lot of shopping in her six weeks here.

The airport is hot and humid, and crowds of people walk about, looking at their watches. I stare at the airplanes in the distance, wondering if I'll ever see the inside of one.

Mimi grabs my arm and hugs me sideways. I've gotten used to the fact that she's a hugger. "Maybe one day you'll come visit me in Houston?" she whispers, as if she's read my mind.

I can't imagine that would ever happen, but I'm quiet. I also never thought I'd be friends with a rich

American girl, or that I could possibly go to school. Impossible, unbelievable things have happened recently, so why couldn't a plane ride be in my future? "Maybe," I whisper, a thrill running down my spine.

Abba and Malik drag up the suitcases, breathing loudly. "You'll be happy to go back to your air-conditioned life, eh, Maryam Ji?" Malik wheezes.

Mimi shrugs. "I guess I will." But I notice she doesn't mind the heat as much as when she first arrived. Everything in Karachi grows on you, like the creeping ivy that lines the boundary walls of Begum Sahiba's house.

"Uncle, please take care of your health, okay?" Mimi tells my abba, and he smiles and nods emphatically to tell her of course he will. Begum Sahiba has already taken charge of his insulin injections, sending him to her own doctor and making sure his diabetes is under control.

Malik immediately begins to give him advice about what foods to eat. "My cousin gobbles down ten jamun every day to keep his diabetes in check," he tells Abba, who waves his concern away.

There's a cough behind us, and everyone turns. I put my hand to my mouth. It's Mimi's father, standing like a lost puppy about ten yards away. A sheen of sweat lines his forehead, and his golden hair glints in the sun.

Mimi runs to him and hugs him tightly, then waves

to her mother with a pleading face.

"What is that man doing here?" Begum Sahiba whispers, her eyes round behind her glasses.

Sahib Ji puts his arm around her. "Just let them be. It's good for Mimi to know her father."

We watch as Samia Ji stands straight like a rod next to her daughter and Tom Scotts Sahib. I can't see her face, but I imagine she's shooting laser eyes at him. Still, there's no fighting, and Mimi's smile is almost as blinding as the sun. I suppose Samia Ji surprised Mimi just like Begum Sahiba surprised me. Alhamdolillah.

Tom Scotts Sahib is a brave man to come here and also smart to leave quickly. He gives Mimi one last hug and kisses the top of her head in exactly the same way as Abba kisses mine, before walking away.

"Did you see my dad? He's going to New York next week, and he says he'll keep in touch with me. Can you believe that?" Mimi can't stop talking when she gets back to us. I roll my eyes at her, but we clasp hands to share the excitement. She's finally looking forward to going back home, because for the first time, home includes her father.

Samia Ji checks her watch, so I know it's time to say goodbye. Begum Sahiba hugs Samia Ji over and over, asking, "When will you come visit us again?" in a cracked voice very unlike her. Sahib Ji mutters and wipes his eyes with his handkerchief, acting like he's wiping sweat, but we all know it's really tears. I feel my eyes soften, and I blink rapidly.

"Don't worry, Nana and Nani," Mimi jumps in with a huge smile. "I'll make sure we come back again soon!" She's wearing her poop emoji T-shirt again, not bothering to cover it up with a cardigan this time. They all hug once more, and then the two Americans wave and walk away, dragging their suitcases behind them.

I watch them go, Abba standing next to me with his arm over my shoulder. Suddenly, Mimi stops and runs back to me. She's got her silver phone in her hand. "Take this, so we can send each other pictures and messages. Nana will make sure the bill gets paid each month, so you don't have to worry about that."

I hug the phone to my chest and watch her skip away to her mother with a final wave and a cheeky grin. I hug it all the way home on Abba's motorcycle, my dupatta wrapped around it tightly. It beeps at night when I'm cooking dinner, Jammy playing next to me with the new cars Mimi sent him. I check the screen. It's my first ever message from Mimi, filled with emojis and smiley faces. *Goodbye, Karachi. Here I come, Houston.*

AUTHOR'S NOTE

I was born in the city of Karachi and lived there until my emigration to the United States at the age of twenty-two. Karachi was my home for a long time, but more than that it was a living space, a character in the drama that was my life. It's a city one can't really forget. I've visited many times in the last few decades to see family and friends, to roam its streets and sample its foods, to meet its people. Each time, another layer has unpeeled, and another face of Karachi has been revealed to me.

The most interesting thing happened with my last trip, however. My children—American-born citizens—accompanied me to their grandmother's house, and their reaction to Karachi was so different from my own. I witnessed their attraction to the motherland they'd never known, their repulsion toward the poverty around them, and their difficulty in communicating in a language they should know, but don't. At the time, my son was slightly older than Mimi and Sakina, and my daughter slightly younger.

We visited many of the same places Mimi and Sakina visited. My kids sat on a camel, marveled at the white mausoleum, wandered through the malls, and heard the azaan multiple times. My daughter was upset at the sight of beggars, and my son frustrated at the slowness of the internet. But they also loved being in a place where everyone looked like them, where they didn't have to worry about standing out. Through my children's eyes, I saw Karachi from an outsider's perspective, and I couldn't help but write down what I was witnessing.

Karachi is an old site, much older than the country of Pakistan. Alexander the Great camped nearby while preparing to march to Babylon. Muslim armies under Muhammad bin Qasim conquered it in the early eighth century. It passed from ruler to ruler over hundreds of years. My favorite part of Karachi's modern history is this: a fisherwoman named Mai Kolachi settled there after her husband's disappearance in a storm, thereby creating a small, fierce community that came to be named Kolachi. From there, it grew into the bustling megacity Karachi is today.

The British captured Karachi in 1843, and the city flourished as a harbor and seaport. In 1878, a railway line connected Karachi to the rest of the British Empire in India, and many of its famous British-era buildings were built at that time. The Quaid-e-Azam, Muhammad Ali Jinnah, was born in Karachi in 1876. Mimi and Sakina learn about the founder of Pakistan when they visit his mausoleum during one of their sightseeing trips.

When the British finally left India, and Pakistan was

created in 1947, Karachi became the new country's capital. It remained so until 1960. It is still the largest and most vibrant city of the nation, the financial and trade center, and the most exciting place to be.

This novel is my love letter to Karachi, a way to lay bare its many complexities and beauties. Much has changed as the decades have passed, and every time I visit, there is something new to discover. But the atmosphere is unchanged, and I hope I've done justice to my memories. Dear Mai Kolachi, you laid the foundations of something very special, and I will never forget this city.

—Saadia

GLOSSARY

(All words are in Urdu unless otherwise stated.)

abba: Father

alhamdolillah: All praise to God (Arabic)

allahu akbar: God is greater (Arabic)

amma/ammi: Mother

asr: Late afternoon prayer (Arabic)

assalamu alaikum: May peace be on you (Arabic)

azaan/adhaan: Call to prayer

badmaash: Hooligan, gangster

basmati: Variety of rice popular in South Asia

begum: A lady of high rank

beta: Son; child

biryani: A spicy rice dish with meat or vegetables

bun kabab: A sandwich with shallow-fried meat-and-lentil patty, egg, onions, and other ingredients

chaat: Snack food made with a mixture of yogurt, boiled potato, and spices

chai: Tea

charpai: A bed made of rope webbing instead of a mattress

daal: Lentils

dupatta: Long scarf worn by women as part of the shalwar kameez ensemble

Eid: Festival or celebration (Arabic)

fajr: Dawn prayer (Arabic)

gharara: Formal outfit worn by women, consisting of tunic and flared pants gathered at the waist

ghee: Clarified butter

gol gappay: A common street snack of round, hollow, fried shells filled with tamarind water.

goonda: Hooligan, miscreant

hai: Oh!

Inshallah: God willing (Arabic)

jamun: A round fruit also known as black plum

ji: An expression added to someone's name to denote respect or affection

Jummah: Friday

kameez: A long tunic worn by men and women; usually paired with shalwar or other pants.

karahi: A thick, circular cooking pot similar to a wok

kheer: Rice pudding

kya haal hai: How are you?

maghrib: Sunset prayer (Arabic)

masala: Spice mix

mazedaar: Delicious

naan: South Asian baked flatbread

nana: Maternal grandfather

nani: Maternal grandmother

oont: Camel

paan: A snack consisting of the betel leaf with other ingredients folded inside, such as chopped areca nut

paratha: Layered flat bread either fried or sautéed in oil

pithu: A traditional South Asian game called seven stones

pulao: A non-spicy rich dish with meat or vegetables

roti: Thin, round flat bread made with whole flour

rickshaw: A small vehicle used as transport; may be pulled manually or driven with a motor

sahib: Master

sahiba: Mistress

salaam: Peace (Arabic)

shalwar: Baggy pants worn by men and women

shami kabab: Minced meat and lentil patty

shukriya: Thank you

tiffin: A metal box used for carrying lunch

tikka boti: Barbecued meat cubes

ulloo-ka-patha: Son of an owl; used as an insult

wa alaikum assalam: And peace be upon you as well (Arabic)

zeera: Cumin

ACKNOWLEDGMENTS

I suppose I should say thanks first and foremost to my mother's knees, which became arthritic and caused her pain, leading to a surgery that required my presence as caretaker. Thanks to that surgery, I dragged my kids halfway across the world in the middle of a sweltering summer to be with their nani. But of course if you know me, you know I was working most of the time. My latest trip to Pakistan was special not only because of my mom's knees, but because it led to this book.

My husband and kids must be acknowledged in all my endeavors, because they give me the space and encouragement to write at a frantic, possibly neurotic pace. This book could easily have been dedicated to all the dinners I did not cook.

My agent, Kari Sutherland, is amazing, and my editor, Rosemary Brosnan, is a dream to work with. I learn so much from these two fantastic women. The entire team at HarperCollins is wonderful to work with. Thank you for taking such good care of my book baby.

A few of my writer friends gave me excellent feedback on this book: Uma Krishnaswami, Dana Mele, and Diane Magras, to name a few. Thank you for your support and gentle guidance. Thank you for reminding me why my culture's stories matter.

And finally, the city of Karachi. Surely, it deserves thanks for being the incredible place it is, for making me fall in love with it even when I thought I hated it, and for being the perfect backdrop for this book. May you always be the City of Lights.

Turn the page for a peek at Saadia Faruqi's *Yusuf Azeem Is Not a Hero*, a novel about a boy struggling to understand identity, grief, and how to stand up for what's right.

1

You suck.

The paper lay faceup on the locker floor. White lined notebook paper. Black ink.

Yusuf blinked and read it again. *You suck.*

He wasn't sure if the paper was meant for him or was left over by the last person to use locker 130A. He looked at the other kids walking around, smiling and high-fiving. The student lockers in the south hallway of Frey Middle School were painted blue. Not a light sky blue, which everyone knew was for babies, but a deep grayish blue. A color that announced "Welcome to middle school!" without being cheesy.

Just a few seconds ago, Yusuf had been thrilled at opening his locker for the first time. Lockers were for big kids. They meant something more than storage: they meant you were old enough. He'd been grinning as he'd spun the dial carefully to make sure he got the numbers right. Seven zero two zero. Easy. He'd already memorized the combination written on the class schedule he'd been emailed the night before. That was also a middle school thing, apparently. An email account from the school, where he'd now get school announcements directly. His username was YUSUF_AZEEM, it said on the schedule, right next to the locker code.

Yusuf Azeem. Son of the famous Mohammad Azeem from A to Z Dollar Store on Marbury Street.

And now this. He pushed his glasses higher up his nose. Then he looked down and studied the inside of the locker. *You suck.* The paper made everything go quiet, like a movie suddenly on mute. He bent his head and studied the paper the way he studied a new LEGO instruction manual. The K had a flourish that turned into a long, straight line. The Y had a curl, as if the writer had tried to learn cursive but had given up.

His breathing slowed. The hair on the back of his neck bristled. What should he do?

Only for a minute, though. Someone jostled his side lightly as they passed. The world began to move again.

Yusuf let out his breath in a whoosh. He decided the paper was a mistake. Students were streaming into the gym from the hallways, their faces bent to their schedules to figure out where to go. Nobody could have decided he sucked in the ten minutes since the school bell rang. It had to be a mistake. Middle school was going to be awesome. He knew that 2021 was going to be his year. Cafeteria food. Chromebooks. Robotics club. This blue-gray locker.

And most important, the annual Texas Robotics Competition. Yusuf couldn't wait for things to get started. He'd been preparing for the TRC his entire life.

It was time for life to get interesting.

Principal Williamson was short and energetic, with bouncy brown hair tied in a ponytail and her face thick with makeup that shone under the gym lights. She wore a silky blue jumpsuit with sequins on the collar and held a microphone in her hands like a deejay.

At least, that was what Yusuf thought deejays dressed like. You needed to go to Houston or Austin for an actual concert, and Amma and Abba would faint if he ever suggested it. Good Muslim kids didn't go to concerts, they'd say, frowning with disappointment.

Danial had found a space on the floor all the way in the far corner of the gym. "Over here!" He waved to Yusuf.

Yusuf sank down into the empty spot next to his best

friend. "Why didn't you walk to school with me?" he grumbled, fiddling with his glasses.

Danial shrugged, his floppy black hair spilling onto his forehead and around his ears. "My mom wanted to drop me off, since it was the first day and all. I think she just wanted to show off her new Jeep."

Yusuf squished the tiny spark of envy inside his chest. Danial's parents were computer engineers, and they worked in the new Exxon regional headquarters about twenty miles out of town. This was his mom's third new car since Danial was born.

"Come home with me after school?" Danial asked. "I got a new LEGO set we can build together."

Yusuf stared straight ahead at Principal Williamson. She stood on a little wooden stage, checking her microphone, whispering, "Hello? Hello?"

"Can't," he replied reluctantly. "My mamoo is visiting at dinner."

"The uncle from Houston? He's cool."

Yusuf didn't say that a LEGO set sounded cooler. That was a given. But Uncle Rahman came a close second.

"Did you set up your email yet?" Danial continued. "I'm thinking of changing my username to legomaniac2021."

Yusuf didn't know you could change your username.

Why would anyone want to do that? "I'm okay with mine. Besides, what will you do next year? Change it to 2022?"

Danial obviously hadn't thought of that. He shrugged like he didn't care, but his face was scrunched up as if he'd swallowed a pickle.

"This is so childish," he complained, nodding to the front of the gym.

"What? It's middle school. It's what they do on the first day." Yusuf was sure this welcome assembly was a time-honored tradition. At least, that was what the email last night had said.

The sound system crackled, making them jump. "Helloooo, boys and girls, welcome to Frey Middle! I'm your principal, Mrs. Williamson, and I'll be your pilot for the duration of your flight."

There was silence. A few groans.

Principal Williamson looked around with a pained face. "Wow, tough crowd! Okay, no worries. I realize it's the first day of middle school for some of you, and you're probably still in summer vacation mode. Not a problem! Now, let me go over some rules before y'all head on to your classrooms. . . ."

Yusuf tried to listen to the rules. He really did. There were easy ones, like no running in the hallways, and no fighting ever. Wandering the school without a hall pass was the biggest crime a kid could commit, apparently. There was something about bathroom breaks, and a great deal about the sports teams you could join.

But the note in his locker kept swimming into his vision, until Mrs. Williamson's face resembled a lined notebook paper with black letters on it. "Did you open your locker yet?" he whispered to Danial.

Danial was jotting down the names of all the sports clubs on the palm of his hand. Soccer on Monday. Basketball on Tuesday and Friday. Wrestling on Wednesday. Yoga on Thursday. "Why would anybody choose yoga?" he whispered back. "Yoga is for old ladies."

"Yoga is meditation from ancient India."

"I really don't care. It's for old ladies."

Yusuf decided there was no use arguing. He chewed on the inside of his cheek, then asked again. "Locker?"

"Dude, I didn't even *get* to my locker yet," Danial replied. "I think the last class can still access them in the first week of school."

Yusuf didn't ask how Danial knew this. His father, Mr. Khan, was on the school board, so all sorts of school secrets were probably discussed at their dinner table. A wave of relief washed over Yusuf. The note in his locker could have been left over from the year before. It was meant for somebody else. Maybe someone who actually sucked.

Definitely not Yusuf.

"Okay, who can tell me the three values of Frey Middle School?" shouted Mrs. Williamson, the sequins on her jumpsuit glinting brightly. "The first one starts with a P."

The gym erupted into laughter.

"It's perseverance," whispered Yusuf, but nobody could hear him over the noise.

2

After the assembly was over, Yusuf and Danial stood in the hallway outside the gym comparing class schedules. They weren't in any classes together, which was the worst news. They'd been together ever since kindergarten, except in third grade, which Danial had labeled the Year of Sorrows.

"This is a bad sign," Danial pronounced, pushing his hair out of his eyes. "How will you function without me?"

Yusuf ducked his head to hide his smile. "I'll manage somehow, don't worry."

They were standing right under a big white banner that said WELCOME, NEW STUDENTS! and a smaller black one that said NEVER FORGET—TWENTY

YEARS. Yusuf examined the black one. Twenty years was a very long time to keep remembering something.

Danial hefted his new Star Wars backpack higher on his shoulder. It was so shiny new, it still had the plastic wire of the tag attached to one strap. "I think this will be the middle school of sorrows."

Yusuf looked back at Danial. "Don't be silly. We'll get to see each other in lunch and PE and library."

"Those are all baby classes."

"No, they're not," Yusuf replied cheerfully. Firmly. "They're the most essential classes. Nourishing the body and the brain and the spirit."

"Ugh, you're so positive, it's disgusting."

Yusuf said, "Remember over the summer, how we built LEGO robots and watched Texas News Network with Abba at the store?"

"Man, those were some messed-up news reports on TNN. People hating on anybody who's different," Danial replied. "Why does your dad watch that all the time?"

"He says we should know what's going on around us. Learn about the worst and hope for the best."

Danial chortled. "Yeah, he's always saying that. He should make a poster and hang it over his checkout counter next to that plaque of his. Or maybe even replace that old plaque. It's getting rusty."

"He'll never replace the plaque, not in a million years."

Yusuf started walking. "Anyway, what I'm saying is, that's how we should begin middle school. Learn the worst and hope for the best."

Danial followed, his backbone bent. "I repeat: ugh."

They separated in the hallway outside the gym and went in opposite directions. Yusuf watched for a minute as Danial grew smaller in the distance. "Good luck!" he called out, but Danial was too far away to hear him. He hefted his backpack and walked slowly. *YUSUF_AZEEM reporting for duty!*

Despite his positivity, his stomach was grumbling. Classes without his best friend. A locker with a mean note inside. And it wasn't even nine o'clock in the morning yet. He wished he hadn't eaten the fried eggs Amma had cooked. They always left his mouth feeling greasy.

Pretty soon, though, the morning improved, because first period was science.

Yusuf's science teacher was Mr. Parker, which was the best news on the class schedule. Mr. Parker had been voted Teacher of the Year seven years in a row, his name proudly displayed on a billboard on El Paso Street where the twin buildings of Frey Elementary and Frey Middle stood. The evening news had sent a reporter to interview him this past summer. That was how Yusuf knew the teacher held a degree in chemistry from the University of Houston, had two teenage sons, and liked strawberry shortcake ice cream.

"Science is going to be very interesting this year, kids," Mr. Parker announced, his clipped brown mustache stretching with his smile. "We'll do some cool science experiments right here in the classroom. How much do you know about slime?"

A few of the kids groaned, as if Mr. Parker was being cheesy. Yusuf wanted to smile back at him, but he hesitated. Maybe smiling at teachers in middle school was frowned upon by the others? He sneaked a peek at the rest of the class. There were a few kids he already knew, like Madison Ensley, who was always picked line leader in every elementary grade class, and Cameron Abdullah, who wore one shiny earring and made the weirdest jokes. Of course, in a town the size of Frey, there were hardly ever any new kids. They all knew one another.

Mr. Parker was writing safety instructions on the whiteboard with a blue dry-erase marker. Number one, follow rules. Number two, notify the teacher IMMEDIATELY if there's a fire or a spill. Number three, wear safety goggles for lab activities.

Yusuf thought the rules looked like code. Everybody knew programming code came in steps, or sequences. His hands itched to write some code, but he forced himself to copy down Mr. Parker's safety rules instead.

When he looked up, his eyes met Cameron's, aka Kamran. Cameron wiggled his eyebrows and rolled his eyes at Mr. Parker. "Boring!" he mouthed.

Yusuf shook his head. Mr. Parker's safety instructions might not be exciting, but they were essential. On his last visit to Frey, Uncle Rahman had told Yusuf about a lab technician in his hospital who mixed some chemicals wrong. Not only was there a mini lab explosion, but the tech's eyebrows had gotten singed because he forgot to wear goggles. The image made Yusuf grin. He could just imagine the poor lab assistant without eyebrows.

"Glad my safety rules are making you laugh, young man."

Yusuf gulped and looked carefully at Mr. Parker. "Uh, I was thinking of something I'd heard," he confessed. He tapped the frame of his glasses with a finger.

"About . . . ?"

Yusuf had no intention of starting sixth grade on the wrong foot. He ducked his head. "Nothing, sir. I'm sorry."

"What's your name?" came the dreaded question.

For a split second, Yusuf thought about using an American version of his name. Joseph? Joe? How hard could it be? After all, Kamran had managed the transformation into Cameron in fifth grade without any trouble. It was the first day of middle school. He could do this, if he wanted.

No. Abba always said, "Be proud of who you are. Be proud of the name and everything that comes with it." He took a deep breath and said, enunciating each syllable clearly, "Yusuf Azeem, sir."

Then Mr. Parker said, "Well, Yusuf Azeem sir, please listen carefully, because your first assignment will be on these safety rules."

Yusuf stared at Mr. Parker, and Mr. Parker stared back solemnly for six whole seconds before turning to the whiteboard. Cameron made a shocked face with both hands over his cheeks and mouthed, "Busted!"

Yusuf stared straight ahead for the rest of the class, focusing all his energy like a laser beam at Mr. Parker's shiny forehead.